SYMBOLUM VENATORES

WAR OF THE TWO KINGDOMS

Also available in eBook.

Symbolum Venatores: The Gabriel Kane Collection and *Hod* are available separately in paperback and eBook.

Published by Dark Titan Entertainment.

Dark Titan Extended is a branch of Dark Titan Entertainment.

First Printing 2020.

Paperback ISBN: 978-1-7359429-3-3
eBook ISBN: 978-1-7359429-4-0

darktitanentertainment.com

WORKS BY TY'RON W. C. ROBINSON II

BOOKS

DARK TITAN UNIVERSE SAGA

MAIN SERIES

Dark Titan Knights
The Resistance ⊠rotocol
Tales of the Scattered
Tales of the ⊠ uminous
Day of Octagon
Crossbreed
Heaven's Called

Forthcoming
The Resistance/Protectors War
Underworld
Magicks and Mysticism

SPIN-OFFS

In A Glass of Dawn: The Casebook of
Travis Vail
Maveth: Bloodsport

Forthcoming
The Curse of The Mutant-Thing
Trail of Vengeance
War of The Thunder Gods

THE HAUNTED CITY SAGA

The Legendary Warslinger: The Haunted City I
Battle of Astolat: A Haunted City Prequel
Redemption of the Lost: The Haunted City II
Consequences of the Suffering: The Haunted City III (Forthcoming)

SYMBOLUM VENATORES

Symbolum Venatores: The Gabriel Kane Collection
Hod: A Symbolum Venatores Book
Symbolum Venatores: War of The Two Kingdoms

OTHER BOOKS

Lost in Shadows: A Novel
Lost in Shadows: Remastered
Accounts of The Dead Days
The Book of The Elect
Hallow Sword: Cursed(KOBO Exclusive)
Dark Titan Omnibus: Volume I
The Extended Age Omnibus
Frightened!: The Beginning
EverWar Universe: Knights & Lords
DarK Titan Omnibus: Volume 2 (Forthcoming)

SYMBOLUM VENATORES
WAR OF THE TWO KINGDOMS

TYRON W. ROBINSON II

CONTENTS

CHAPTER ONE

It is the year 930 BC as the Sovereign Solomon, King of the United Kingdom of Israel had died. Now buried with his father David and his fathers before in the City of David. Now, Rehoboam his son must take his place as he is set to travel to Shechem to be declared the new king of the United Kingdom of Israel.

Over in Egypt, under the *Twenty-Second Dynasty*, known as the Bubastite Dynasty, Jeroboam, the son of Nebat, an Israelite from the Tribe of Ephraim heard the news of Solomon's death and was relieved. Sitting in his home provided by Pharaoh Shishak, the informant also gave him a scroll detailing what's to come. He opened the scroll, beaten as it appeared and read what was written.

"His son will reign in his stead?"

"That is correct."

Jeroboam sealed the scroll and nodded.

"I will have to assemble all of Israel and speak with the new Sovereign. I hope he will not be as austere as was his father."

Jeroboam spoke with Pharaoh Shishak concerning his next motives and actions. Shishak took in Jeroboam's wishes and permitted him to achieve them, but to remember all the acts and rules he taught him while he was in hiding from Solomon. Therefore, Jeroboam gathered all he had with him and he and his wife, Ano left Egypt for Israel to meet the new king.

At the border of Israel and Phistlia, precisely around Gaza, two Philistines were seeking to gain an entry point into the Israelite Kingdom. They saw an access point through the desert grounds.

"If we march through this valley point, we shall be able to invade and conquer without being seen. Without anyone aware."

As the two Philistines spoke, a man came out of the desert. He was alone, dressed in a brown robe and cloak. He appeared rough-looking, lean, but built physique. His face hidden from the mixture of his diadem and the sunlight. The Philistines saw him and slowly reached for their swords. Walking slowly toward the man.

"Are you lost, good man?"

"No." The man said "I am not. I am right where I should be."

"And why have you come here? To this spot?"

The man focused his gaze upon the Philistines. For his presence was of mystery toward them. They couldn't tell whether he was an Israelite or an Egyptian due to the aura around him.

"Because you're seeking to trespass."

"He's one of them!"

The Philistines rushed toward the man and was cut down within seconds by the man's skills with the sword. One of the Philistines remained alive, but mortally wounded by the blade. Backing himself up roughly through the sand and blood as the man approached him slowly. He took small steps. Slow, but steady.

"Who are you?"

"Elrad. A hunter."

Elrad raised up his sword and killed the Philistine. He wiped the blood from his beard with a cloth from the Philistine. He took their bodies and brought them across the border for all the Philistines to see, reminding them of what happens when anyone of their nation crosses the borders.

CHAPTER TWO

In Shechem, Rehoboam arrived and all Israel greeted him with gladness and joy. For their new king had arrived. Also entering the gates of Shechem was Jeroboam and those who accompanied him. They stood out amongst the Children of Israel, yet, they themselves were Israelites besides his wife Ano. As all of Israel gathered to speak with Rehoboam concerning his ruler ship and how it will be done, Elrad entered the gates and stood in the back of the crowd facing Rehoboam. Still cloaked in his robe, he looked out and saw the joy of the Israelites and nodded quietly. Jeroboam stood forward toward Rehoboam in the eyes of the congregation.

"Sovereign Rehoboam." Jeroboam said, coming before the king. "May I speak with you?"

"What have you need to speak to me?"

"It concerns your rule. Will you rule as your father Solomon did? Will you rule over us with grievous intent? Will you put a heavy yoke around our necks as he did? Will you?"

"What would you have me do?"

"Make it lighter. Make the yoke lighter for all Israel's sake. That way, we will know for surely, you are the king Yisra'el truly needs."

Rehoboam nodded, taking in Jeroboam's words. The words were true and Rehoboam knew it. He understood the rule of his father and how it was grievous amongst the Israelites. Rehoboam turned his back to walk away and

Jeroboam reached for his robe.

"Will you make it lighter?" Jeroboam asked again.

Rehoboam stood before the congregation with confidence.

"I will make a decision in three days' time. But, before I do such a great task, I must seek counsel. I believe Yahweh's will may be done. For all of Yisra'el."

Rehoboam walked from the congregation as they began to speak amongst themselves. Voices speaking over voices. Conversations going all around the city of Shechem. Elrad watched the congregation as they spoke concerning Rehoboam and he walked away to a place for himself. Jeroboam walked into the congregation. He hoped Rehoboam would take his plea seriously and make it so. The congregation later departed.

Within the three days, Rehoboam consulted with the old men, those who were under his father's rule. For they saw what had transpired before in a generation and now they must give word to Rehoboam's rule, for the young king is uncertain of what to give the Children of Israel. Should he continue his father's way of rule or should he bring forth a lighter rule, in order for all Israel to be content. Rehoboam sat at the table before the old men, shaking his head. Unable to make a final decision.

"How do you advise me to respond to the people?" Rehoboam asked. "What should I do? Keep my father's rule or bring forth a lighter way?"

"We have a proposition for you, my king." One of the men said.

"Please, I would like to hear it."

"If you would appear to be like a servant to the congregation and serve them, then this day forth, you will answer them according to their desire. Speak good words to them and they shall be your servants forever."

Rehoboam nodded. Taking in the advice from the council.

"Is that what you believe I should do? Make myself a servant in their eyes? So, they would in turn become servants for my sake and the kingdom's?"

"That is what we advise, my king. We know no other alternative. For if you do this, the people will rejoice of your rule once more and contentment will abound by them for all of your rule and your son's rule and his son's."

Rehoboam nodded. "Thank you for your counsel. I will take it under consideration."

The old men showed obeisance toward Rehoboam as they left his sight.

Two days had passed and Rehoboam had yet to make a decision for Israel. He was torn between the advice of the old men and the request from Jeroboam. On the third day, deep in the night, Rehoboam met with some of the younger men within Shechem. For they met in one of the study rooms within the city. One preserved for the king. They came in a sat among Rehoboam, seeing the concern on his face. For he worried about the people and their response to his decision. The older men had already given him direction on what to do, but, he isn't certain of that method.

"What should I do?" Rehoboam asked. "I'm not sure what to do for Israel."

"What did the older men advise you to do?"

"They told me to become a servant amongst the people, to make the rule lighter, and they would in turn become servants to myself and the kingdom."

"I see their reasoning for such advice."

"The people said they want me to make the yoke which my father put upon the lighter. Is that what I should do? Make it lighter and become a servant to the people and they to me?"

"Well, we do have a proposition for you." One had said.

"I would love to hear it." Rehoboam said, sitting up in his chair.

"This you shall speak to the Children of Yisra'el, you shall continue your father's way of rule. When they ask of it once more, tell them your little *finger* shall be thicker than your father's loins."

The second friend entered into the conversation saying, "Now, you shall tell them whereas your father placed upon them a heavy yoke, you shall add to that yoke."

The third friend entered and said, "As your father had chastised them with whips, you shall chastise them with scorpions and straps."

Rehoboam listened carefully to those words spoken by the younger men. He nodded and a glint of a smile appeared on his face.

"Thank you for your advice. I'll consider everything before I speak amongst the congregation."

"It is what friends are for our king."

The younger men left Rehoboam's sight and after the three days had passed he stood in front of the congregation. For they all awaited an answer to their futures. Jeroboam was present for the speaking as was Elrad, who stood in the same place as before. Unlike most of Israel, Elrad was still. Calm. Collective. He neither yelled or frowned as the Israelites were doing in the presence of Rehoboam.

"He's about to speak." A young woman said to Elrad. "I hope he delivers what we asked of him."

"What he gives will be what his father commanded." Elrad said. "He's Solomon's son. He will behave as Solomon behaved to a degree. So, expect what you already know to come."

Rehoboam walked out before the people as they cheered his name, praising Yahweh for their new king. Jeroboam stood in the front of the congregation; his eyes were keen on Rehoboam. Hoping he doesn't make the same mistake his father did.

"Children of Yisra'el, you have asked of me concerning my rule for you all. And after much counsel, I have come to a decision. That decision is clear and final. For I shall not lighten the yoke around your necks."

The congregation mumbled in fear, hearing the words coming from Rehoboam. Jeroboam looked with uncertainty as a hint of anger began brewing within him. Elrad stood watch, sensing the dread coming over the Israelites.

"My father made your yoke heavy and I shall add to that yoke! My father also chastised you all with whips, but I shall chastise you all with scorpions and straps!"

"We didn't ask for this!" A man yelled from the congregation. "You're no better!"

"Oh, I am better." Rehoboam responded. "I am much better. For I am bringing forth my father's rule in greater feats and in greater strengths!"

The older men stood in the congregation, hanging their heads in shame as they knew he took the advice of the younger men, his friends over theirs. For his friends have no wisdom. No experience. They were just doing what they pleased with Rehoboam. Rehoboam left the sight of the Israelites as they echoed in anger, fear, and dread. Elrad watched as Israel was being divided before his eyes. A tragic sight for one in the twelve tribes. Yet, Elrad had remembered a prophecy spoken by Ahijah the Shilonte, stating that such an action would happen, in order to cause Jeroboam to divide the kingdom of Israel. This was all caused by Yahweh. For it was spoken by his prophet.

Elrad walked away from the shouting sprees amongst the Children of Israel. For being separate at was the only way he could obtain any sense of peace within a quickly eroding kingdom.

CHAPTER THREE

All of Israel were grievous and stricken by Rehoboam's words and his desire of rule. Jeroboam appeared before them, giving them comfort and a hope for a brighter future. The way Jeroboam spoke to the congregation had given them a thought, that thought became an idea, and that idea became a possibility. They no longer wanted Rehoboam to be their king and to rule over them. They desired Jeroboam. For his speech and his intent towards Israel.

"What portion do we have in Dawid?" The congregation had asked Rehoboam when in his presence once more. "Neither do we have any inheritance in the son of Jesse?"

"Return to your tents." Rehoboam commanded the congregation. "See to your own tents, Yisra'el!"

The congregation did as Rehoboam commanded and returned to their tents. However, after some time had passed and the anger began to grow amongst the Israelites, they began to separate themselves from Rehoboam and his rule over the kingdom. They demanded to have a new leader to lead them into the future. Most of the Israelites had sided with Jeroboam with only the Children of Judah remaining with Rehoboam. Things were changing. Division was now seen and felt amongst all of Israel. Elrad remained where he stood, in the place of the Tribe of Benjamin.

A time later, Rehoboam remained in the city of Jerusalem and called into his study, Adoniram. Adoniram was over the tribute to Israel and to the kingdom. Adoniram was the son of Abda, a servant of Yahweh. Adoniram respected Rehoboam for his kingship and his place amongst all Israel.

"Adoniram, I send you to Shechem to collect the taxes of the people."

"My sovereign. I believe the people will not give you the taxes you speak of. For they are angry with you. Very wroth."

"Leave that to me. Go and retrieve the taxes and return. We need it done."

Adoniram bowed and left Rehoboam's sight.

For the ten northern tribes dwelled in the northern part of the kingdom, while the tribes of Benjamin and Judah remained in the southern division of the kingdom. The following day, Adoniram made way to Shechem to speak to the congregation and Elrad was there to see him leave. He knew what would happen to Adoniram and only shook his head in shame of Rehoboam's decision.

Adoniram arrived in Shechem and gathered all the Israelites in the city toward him. They knew he was one of Rehoboam's trusty men and they hesitated to hear any words that would come from his mouth. But, they hoped they would be words of change. Words of hope. A lighter hope. The people amongst him were focused. their faces stiff, but still pliable to a degree. The younger generations were only following what seemed popular, whereas the older generations hoped for what was needed.

"King Rehoboam has sent me here to collect your labor

taxes and to be delivered to him this day."

"Taxes?" A man said. "Taxes?! He sends you here so we can give him our wages?!"

"It's his rule. He commands it."

"Here are our wages. We're sure Rehoboam will be pleased."

At that moment, stones began to fly toward Adoniram. Stones coming from the hands of the congregation. Smashing into his face, arms, legs, stomach, and back. He crouched down to avoid more stones. Yet, they were too much. The stones started to fall atop his head, knocking him unconscious with the following stones signaling the killing blow. Such an assault eventually killed Adoniram. In the distance, Rehoboam was present, sitting atop his horse and he witnessed the stoning. He took off, fleeing back to Jerusalem.

After the stoning, Jeroboam came before the people and spoke to them of the change and the comfort he could bring. Something in which Rehoboam will not do. Then, it was settled in the hearts of the people to make Jeroboam the king of the northern tribes of Israel. Jeroboam accepted their request and became their king. In the center of Shechem and banner was made and showcased amongst them people. For in Jerusalem, were banners of a violet menorah. In Shechem, a golden menorah shined. Signifying the divided kingdoms of Israel.

CHAPTER FOUR

Rehoboam returned to Jerusalem and the people of Benjamin and Judah saw the fear in Rehoboam's eyes. He rode back to his dwelling place and immediately called in the elders. He spoke to them of what happened to Adoniram and the elders concluded that Rehoboam speak to the northern tribes and give them what was spoken previously. A lighter rule and a lighter yoke. Be a servant to the people and they shall become your servants. Rehoboam disapproved their recommendations and went into his chambers.

Elrad remained with his people of Benjamin and they kept to themselves. Although the children of Judah desired to speak to the king, he would not hear a word, not even more from the elders, the priests, or his friends. Rehoboam was at a loss. The following days, Rehoboam went out amongst the children of Judah and Benjamin and began rallying up the young men and older for war against the northern tribes. Rehoboam wanted revenge for Adoniram's death and a civil war was his way of receiving it.

Meanwhile, the northern tribes celebrated as Jeroboam was their king. The United Kingdom of Israel was no more.

The Divided Kingdom was born. Rehoboam had gathered all the men he could. A total of eighty-thousand men. All chosen and they were already warriors. Capable of battle. They were prepared to combat the northern tribes. Rehoboam saw this as a way of not only getting his revenge, but uniting the kingdom by force.

Near noon in the day, Elrad stood outside the gates of Jerusalem for he was led by an unseen present. It did not speak to him, only with utterance did it bring him outside the gates. Elrad looked around and only saw the grass, dirt, and trees. As he looked around, he could feel piercing eyes were upon him. Where were they is what he asked himself. Before he could turn back to the city, a black must fell from the sky and attacked him. Clawing at his robes. Elrad fought back, raising his sword and swiping the mist.

"What are you?" Elrad asked.

"You must not live!" The mist spoke. "You must not live!"

The mist swooped down against Elrad with its claws. Elrad continued using his sword to back away the strange mist and before it could reach his robes, Elrad slammed the sword into what appeared to be the mist's head and it collapsed into the grass. Elrad looked closer and knew what he was seeing.

"A djinn?" Elrad said. "Here? Why?"

The djinn was helpless as Elrad went and grabbed a vase. He commanded for the djinn to enter the vase and it obeyed. After the djinn was placed inside the vase, Elrad went out further from Jerusalem and buried it. He returned to the city after and did not speak a word to anyone concerning the djinn, only mediating on the words it spoke to him. He understood those words were indeed referring to him and him alone. As Elrad walked, a cloaked figure stood beside a tree, watching the Benjamite. He figure was hooded, wearing all black. He nodded with a smile showing underneath the hood.

"It is time." He uttered, glaring at Elrad.

CHAPTER FIVE

While Rehoboam prepared all he had to attack the northern tribes of Israel, Shemaiah, a man of Yahweh approached him in his study. His countenance was of urgent concern and Rehoboam could see it.

"My king, I have news."

"What kind of news?" Rehoboam asked. "Is it about Jeroboam? Does it concern the northern tribes? If it does not, you may leave me be."

"It concerns them. It only concerns them."

Rehoboam nodded and sat down. He gestured his hands toward Shemaiah to come forward to the table.

"Please, tell me of this news."

"Yahweh has spoken to me. About the matters of the kingdom and what has come of it."

"What has He said?"

"He says this; thus saith Yahweh, you shall not go up nor shall you fight your brethren. Return every man to his home. For all of this is from me."

Rehoboam laid back in his chair and went into deep thought. Shemaiah stood still. Patiently awaiting a response from the king of Judah. Rehoboam considered he words of Yahweh and waved his hand.

"Very well. As Yahweh speaks, I will obey. I will tell the men to return home."

Shemaiah bowed his head and left the chambers. Rehoboam later went out and spoke to the warriors who were awaiting the notion to head out. Rehoboam told them everything Shemaiah had spoken and they knew it was from Yahweh. They gathered together and obeyed the command, returning home. While everyone was heading home, Shemaiah walked outside, seeing Elrad. He approached him keenly as Elrad turned to face him.

"Good sir." Elrad said. "What do you have need of?"

"I have no needs, son. For, I have come to deliver a message to you."

"A message? Of what sort?"

"Prepare yourself. You'll have a visitor this night and it will change the course of your life. Take heed to these words."

"My life? What do you mean?"

"You will find out when you return home. Right now, take this moment of thought and consider the costs that await you. Although, they are not many, they will become factors that charter your life in the coming age."

"I'm not understanding anything you're telling me."

"By dawn tomorrow, you will understand. You will begin to comprehend."

Elrad was left in confusion as Shemaiah took his leave.

He was not wrong when later in the night, Elrad returned home and discovered a man waiting for him. Cloaked in a rugged and torn black robe. Elrad raised his sword at the man.

"Who are you?"

He removed his hood, revealing his face. Elrad knew the face and sheathed the sword.

"I'm sorry, Prophet. I didn't know it was you."

"You have no need of apologizing, Elrad of Benjamin. You

know who I am."

"I do. You're Iddo the Prophet."

"Then you do know of me."

"Many haven't seen you since Solomon's reign. Why return to the light now? Why come to my home?"

"Because prophecy speaks of you, Elrad."

"Prophecy? I do not understand. I'm just a simple man."

"Prophecy most often requires simple men."

Elrad sat down and Iddo in front. Iddo began to lay out the details to him slowly. Iddo was not seen since the death of Solomon, due to him going into self-isolation of a spiritual matter. Iddo informed Elrad he has been told to come out of the shadows to speak to Elrad about his future. His future in being part of a greater cause.

"There is an Order if you will, which exists. Many have not heard of it and many never will. They have spoken and you are one of them. One in a generation."

"What kind of Order is this? Is it like the Levities?"

"In a manner. However, the Levities aren't qualified to attest to some of the actions one must endure to become one with this Order."

"This Order, does it have a name?"

"In our tongue, it is called the *Oth Tsayad*. Elsewhere, it has many names. In times to come, a certain name."

"*Hunter's Sign*." Elrad said.

"You now see why they have chosen you to join them."

"What is their purpose? Hunt for sport and deliver the goods to the people?"

"What the Oth Tsayad do is far from the natural world. You see Elrad, the hunters target a particular kind of source. As I recall, you came into conflict with one earlier this day."

Elrad took the moment and remembered. The djinn outside the walls. The vase. The burial. All was put in commotion for this moment. All planned. All known.

"You sent that thing?"

"I did not. It appeared because things are changing. Strange entities are appearing all across Yisra'el. Ever since the kingdom was ripped in two, unusual things have occurred. Now, the Oth Tsayad has called you to stop these occurring events and place a balance within the land of Yisra'el."

"And how am I to stop these supernatural events with a basic sword?"

"I've seen others defeat far more powerful forces with a stick and a purse. I believe you can manage. You took down the djinn, which escaped from one of Solomon's temples. It was a gift from one of his wives."

"His wives are what is responsible for the time we're living in. his love for women exceeded him greatly. All into his old years."

"You speak odd of your former king?" Iddo asked. "A son of Dawid? A man after Yahweh's own heart?"

"I do not. I only speak the truth to the acts which have occurred and what are occurring. His son, Rehoboam is now seeking war with Jeroboam and the northern tribes. I desire not to fight my brethren, however, if the call comes, I will obey. For I am an Israelite from the Tribe of Benjamin. A servant of Yahweh."

"Then, you will do what I speak to you."

"What have you for me?"

"There are three trials. You must complete them and I will return to you once they're done."

"I see. Will this make Israel better for the people?"

"It will." Iddo confirmed. "In time."

"What must I do?"

"First trial requires two places of water. You must first dip yourself into the Sea of Lot ten times. This is for the northern tribes who have sided with Jeroboam. Then, you must go and travel to the Kinneret and dip yourself in its waters two times. This is for the tribes of Benjamin and Judah."

Elrad nodded.

"What must I do after that?"

"I will meet you at the shores of Kinneret and tell you there. Take a moment to pray tonight and head out in the morning. Your life changes this day."

Iddo left Elrad's home and he obeyed the words of Iddo. He prayed and took some rest. In the morning, Elrad grabbed what he needed and lastly grabbed his sword. He took a horse and left Jerusalem, beginning his trials of the Oth Tsayad.

CHAPTER SIX

In the middle of the ongoing civil war amongst Rehoboam and Jeroboam, Elrad began his trials of the Oth Tsayad. First heading out toward the southeast to the Dead Sea. There, he stopped his horse, jumped off, and walked toward the salty water. The stench of the air was filled with the smell of salt. Its strong odor moved through the air from the gust of the wind. Elrad removed his robes and diadem, walking into the sea. He went as far as he could and dove underwater. Elrad chose to remain there for seven seconds. Afterwards, he arose and repeated the same tactic nine more times, following the words of Iddo the Prophet. Once he was complete, he dried himself off and quickly made travels up north.

Entering the area now belonging to Jeroboam and his kingdom. The Israelites of the northern tribes looked at Elrad with funny looks. They knew he was a Benjamite and believed he was confused on his goings. One older man approached Elrad on his horse. He looked concern about Elrad's doings in the northern kingdom.

"Why are you here?"

"I'm heading north. To the Kinneret."

"For what purpose?" The older man asked. "Why go there?"

"It's of urgent matter. I cannot speak of it any further."

"Our king must know you're here."

"He'll find out soon enough."

Elrad rode through the town of Adam, following the river leading toward the Sea of Galilee. He did not stop for food, drink, or rest. Elrad was focused on the cause and only death would cease his actions. Neither was his horse tired nor hungry. After the travels, he reached the Sea of Galilee and entered the water as a few fisherman looked at him strangely.

"What's he doing?" A fisherman said to another.

"Probably drunk is all. You know those types."

Elrad dipped himself two times and arose from the sea, returning to shore. The fishermen watched as he dried himself off and put his garments back on. One fisherman approached Elrad after he dressed himself.

"Good man, why go and dip in the water two times?"

"It's for the tribes of Benjamin and Judah. A sign of things to come."

"What kind of sign? A deliverance from this nonsensical war or will Yahweh return to us once again and reunite us all under one kingdom?"

"I do not have the answers you seek. Perhaps, when the time comes, you will know them."

The fisherman walked away and as Elrad turned around, Iddo was there. Elrad was startled at the prophet's sudden presence.

"How did you do that?"

"No need to know. I see you've completed the first trial."

"I did. Never expected I'll be in much water for the past two days."

"However, you've completed the trial. Good things are coming you way. Right now, I suggest you take a moment to rest. The second trial awaits you."

"What is this second trial? I should be inclined to know."

Iddo nodded and stepped forward toward Elrad.

"The second trial requires you to travel to *Har Tzion*. When you get there, a messenger will speak to you concerning the true purpose of these trials. Afterwards, you must go to *Qadesh Barne'a*, where reports have come out of a witch hiding out in the wilderness of the lands. Exterminate her and I'll be there to tell you of your third and final trial."

"And what comes after all of this? When I've done everything there is to be done?"

"You will find out. When the trials are complete."

"Get some rest, warrior. You need it for the journey ahead." Iddo turned and walked away.

Elrad went to an inn and rested for the night. Upon the brink of dawn, he arose and traveled to Mount Zion. During his travels, he continued to hear the people talk of Jeroboam's plans to face Rehoboam. The war was still going, but Elrad was focused on the trials more than the civil war. Time later, Elrad made it to the mountain and looked around. Walking across the land.

"Where's this messenger Iddo spoke of?" Elrad questioned.

Elrad turned around to see anyone. No one was near his location or in his eyesight of distance. However, when he turned and looked back, he found himself in the presence of a celestial being. Its power was strong enough to cause Elrad to fall to his knees. Elrad blocked the bright light with his shield, attempting to raise his head. He could not. He was losing much strength.

"What is this?!" Elrad yelled.

"Do not fear, Elrad. I come with no harm."

Elrad paused as the energy lowered and stood up, seeing

the figure in full, dressed in linen with its loins girded with fine gold from Uphaz. Elrad knew what he was looking at and was astonished. The figure stood around Elrad's same height, but knowingly lowered it to speak to the Benjamite face-to-face. Its body was like beryl and its face appeared like lightning. The eyes were like lamps of fire. The arms and feet were like polished brass. When the figure spoke, its voice moved like a voice of a multitude. A voice of many.

"You come from the heavens. A messenger from Yahweh."

"I come from afar. Yes."

"Why? Have you come to take my life?"

"No. your time is not close. I've come for a very specific purpose."

"Does this purpose have anything to do with the Oth Tsayad?" Elrad asked. "These trials told to me by Iddo?"

"Yes. What Iddo has told you is true. You have been chosen by the Oth Tsayad to become their hunter for the land of Israel."

"Why me?"

"Because you have the qualifications of a remnant."

"So I have been told." Elrad mocked. "What have you to tell me?"

"Your future is set and your path is clear. This order of hunters. You shall bear their sign upon the sigil of the tribe of Benjamin. Every nation upon the earth requires a hunter of this order. There is no discrimination. You have been chosen for Israel's sake."

"Is this Yahweh's will?"

"You will discover that when you've completed all there is."

Elrad shook his head. He was annoyed by all he was hearing. More so by Iddo's words regarding the trials. Elrad is an obedient man and nodded.

"What must I do next?"

"Qadesh Barne'a awaits you. Help the people down there with the witch. Rid her from the land and Iddo will be there to tell you what's to come."

The messenger went away and Elrad sighed, returning to his horse for the ride down to Kadesh Barnea. Meanwhile, as Elrad went about the trials, Jeroboam was building and preparing the northern tribes for war. However, he thought to himself, in his own heart if the kingdom should return unto the house of David, then the people will go and sacrifice to Yahweh in Jerusalem and the people would side with Rehoboam, leaving him to himself. Alone and outnumbered. They would indeed kill him. Jeroboam did not want this and thought of another way to keep the people under his rule.

Jeroboam went ahead and built up Shechem in Mount Ephraim. He chose to dwell there. To live out his days in Shechem. Also, he built Penuel during these days. Jeroboam took the counsel of what to do to keep his rule remaining. The counsel he had with him commanded him of such ways and he agreed to them whatever the cost. It began later that night, the same night of Elrad's first trial, Jeroboam took gold and made two calves. He presented them to the northern tribes in Shechem for all to see. The people were confused. Some were curious. Others were happy to see something shining in their gaze.

"Is it too much for you to return to Jerusalem? Behold this day, your gods, O' Yisra'el! These are the gods which brought you up from the land of Egypt!"

The people clamored and cheered on Jeroboam for bringing these gods of gold to them. They celebrated that night as Jeroboam brought one calf and set it in the city of

Bethel. He placed the other one in the city of Dan. What he had done was bring upon sin over the people as they went and began worshiping the gods of gold. His next move of ruler ship was making priests out of the lowest of the people in the region and building a house of high places.. This is a strike due to the fact the lowest of the people were not sons of Levi.

Elrad arrived in Kadesh Barnea and saw how the people moved with fear. He rode through the small area keenly. The people questioned who he was and why was he in their sight. Elrad called for the leader of the land and he appeared before him. Elrad asked about the sightings of the witch and the leader told him of the events. How the witch appeared from deep within the wilderness, striking those who traveled alone on the roads. Elrad gestured the witch didn't come for him. The leader proposed he wait for the night and head out into the wilderness, for the witch will make herself known. Elrad agreed to the proposal and rested in Kadesh Barnea for the remainder of the day.

The night had come and Elrad went straight forth into the wilderness. Sword in hand. Shield on the opposite arm. He walked out into the quietness of the forest. Only the sound of chirping could be heard and a cool whistle of the wind. As he walked further, a brushing sound acme from the trees behind him. He turned, looking up. There was nothing. The brushing continued to the point where it could be heard all around him. Elrad shrugged his shoulders, taking out a torch from his side and lighting it. The fire lit up the area and it brought out what he came for.

"Ah." Elrad said. "There you are."

The witch looked very disgruntled. Her clothing was torn as if ripped by lions or bears. Her hair was frizzy, dry, and grey as a rain cloud. her face appeared leathery and her eyes looked as if she was already dead. She stared at Elrad and saw the fire, letting out a loud screech. Elrad dropped the torch, covering his ears as the witch attacked him. Clawing against the shield. Elrad shoved her back and swiped the sword, cutting her left arm from the elbow down. She yelled and went for another attack. This time with such strength, she threw Elrad into the tree behind him.

"What was that?!" Elrad questioned.

The witch came for another attack. Clawing, yelling, and shoving Elrad across the forest. He fell backwards several times before standing up and attacking back. The witch backed up a few feet from Elrad and rushed him. Elrad took the shield and tripped the witch, then used his sword to impale her into the ground. The impact caused the witch to slow down as she struggled to stand up, but the sword was too far deep between her and the ground. The fact she was not dead caused concern for Elrad.

"Is this what I'm meant to do?" Elrad asked. "To find and kill things such as you?"

Elrad knelt down toward the witch's face, seeing her undead appearance and her cold eyes. Elrad hung his head down.

"I'm sorry this happened to you. Whomever you were."

Elrad stood up, holding the witch down with his foot as he pulled the sword from her back. He raised it up over her as she continued to struggle. It appeared whatever strength she had was gone. She was helpless.

"You've caused enough harm to the living."

Elrad slashed the sword, decapitating the witch. The fight was over and Elrad sighed with tiredness in his breath. Afterwards, he took the body of the witch and burned it. For he believed one such as her should not receive the proper burial, due to her animal-like appearance and behavior. Elrad felt there was something spiritual about her and not in a benevolent form. Sheathing his sword and setting his shield to his back, he walked away as he body burned to ash.

Over in Bethel, Jeroboam called for a feast to be held in the eighth month on the fifteenth day. The feast was similar to the one in Judah. Jeroboam brought forth an offering and gave it unto the alter. He went and done the same in Bethel. Sacrificing the calves, he made. He commanded the priests he made of the high places to go and remain in Bethel. Later in the early portion of the night, a man of Yah came to Bethel from Judah. He had a word for Jeroboam and his current actions. The man of Yah found Jeroboam standing by the alter, burning incense.

"O' altar! Altar! Thus saith Yahweh!, behold a child shall be born unto the house of Dawid, Josiah by name and upon him shall he offer the priests of the high places to burn incense upon you and men's bones shall be burnt upon you!"

The man of Yah gave a sign that same day.

"This is the sign which Yahweh has spoken! Behold, the altar shall be rent and the ashes which are upon it shall be poured out!"

Jeroboam stood and took in the words of the man of Yah. Listening closely and meditating upon them carefully. Jeroboam went to remove his hand, but he could not. He looked at his hand and saw it became one with the altar. Dried up. He pulled and wrenched. Nothing worked. His hand was part of the altar now. The man of Yah was not troubled by Jeroboam's sudden response. He was calm. Peaceful. Jeroboam turned to the man of Yah immediately, looking at him and his hand upon the altar.

"Intreat the face of Yahweh at this moment and pray for me. Pray that my hand may be restored once again."

The man of Yah listened and besought Yahweh and the king's hand was restored. He hand was as it once was. Jeroboam thanked the man of Yah.

"Come home with me, good sir." Jeroboam said, entreating the man of Yah. "You should receive some refreshment. I must reward you for the restoration of my hand."

The man of Yah responded saying, "If you will give me half of your house, I will not go with you. Neither shall I eat bread or drink water in this place."

"Why not?" Jeroboam asked. "I seek to reward you for restoring my hand."

"It was charged to me by the word of Yahweh." The man said. "He commanded me to eat no bread, drink no water, and not to turn again by the same way I came in."

"What will you do now?" Jeroboam wondered. "I desire to know."

The man of Yah nodded.

"I'm sure you do."

The man of Yah turned from Jeroboam and went another way. As he did not return the same way he came into Bethel.

CHAPTER SEVEN

Elrad returned to his home, smelling of a distant smoke. Inside of the home, Iddo waited. Elrad set his weapons down near the entrance and went for some water at the table. Taking a moment to settle after the journey, he sat down in front of Iddo. His face was keened. He was also tired. Weary from the battle.

"You've completed the task?" Iddo asked.

"The banshee is dead. Burned to ash."

"Then, you are ready."

"As ready as I'll ever be."

"Don't be in such manner to yourself. You will need the rest for this."

"I am to fight something else? Something similar to the witch? Another djinn? Demons?"

"No. There will be no fighting in this final trial. You will be spared from that."

"What is the final trial?" Elrad wondered. "I'm curious to know."

"The final trial is very simple. Go forth and speak to the kings of Judah and Israel. Both of them."

"Speak to the kings? In the middle of a civil war?"

"It is what must be done. For all of Yisra'el and for the Oth Tsayad."

"And what shall I tell the kings? Should I give them word

regarding this order hidden in the shadows? Or should I grant them advice on ending and settling this war of theirs?"

Iddo stood up from his chair and walked toward the opposite table, pouring himself a cup of water. He returned to his seat and drank. Elrad awaited word from Iddo's mouth.

"Go north and ask for a word with Jeroboam. Speak to him first. There, you will learn more than what meets the eye."

"More? What does Jeroboam know that I must know?"

"You will find out when you're in his presence."

"And what of Rehoboam?"

"Speak to him after you've had word with Jeroboam."

"Does he know something as well? Something regarding this Order?"

"Your talk with Rehoboam is about Y'israel and only Y'israel. It's past, present, and future."

Iddo finished the water and stood up from the chair, walking toward the door. He stopped and looked back at Elrad with a smile on his face. Yet, his eyes were focused on the mission.

"Get some rest and head north on the morrow. When you speak with Jeroboam, you will be astounded to what awaits all of life to come."

"I'll do my best."

Elrad rested and the following day, he traveled north, upon reaching the Shechem, Elrad is informed by word of mouth throughout the city that Jeroboam is currently placed in Penuel. Elrad comprehended the changes as to Jeroboam's different way of ruling. Elrad traveled to Penuel and there, he was confronted by soldiers. Four of them, two wielding swords and the others wielding javelins.

"Stop yourself!" A soldier yelled.

"I come to speak with King Jeroboam. It is of great urgency."

"Who sent you?"

"A man of Yah."

The soldiers took a pause and stood aside as Elrad passed through and entered the homestead of Jeroboam. Upon his entry, being led by the soldiers, Jeroboam was sitting in his study, reading a scroll. Elrad stepped foot at the door and Jeroboam's head went up with speed. He saw the figure at the door and stood from the desk.

"Who are you?"

"I am Elrad of Benjamin. I've been sent here by a man of Yah to deliver urgent words."

"A Benjamite? Here in the north? You aren't afraid of what the children of Judah might do or what your own Benjamites might say?"

"I care not for words or actions of the uniformed. I am here by the words of Iddo the Prophet. He told me to meet you."

"Iddo." Jeroboam uttered under his breath. "Ah. Iddo. The Seer."

"You are aware then?"

"As I'll ever be. How is he?"

"He's well. How are you aware of him?"

"He's the one who warned Solomon of my coming and what I was prophesized to do. Now, I look out and I see it has come to pass. But, tell me, Benjamite, why has he sent you here to speak to me and for what cause?"

"To learn of your upbringings and how you prepared for all of this. The war of the two kingdoms. Your decision to go against Rehoboam. The knowledge you gained."

"You seek to know where my wisdom came from?"

"I do."

"And why should I tell you my upbringing? What would someone of your stature do with the knowledge I have obtained?"

"I would use such knowledge for greater causes. Every cause that pertains to all of Y'israel and to Yahweh."

"I see. You're a loyal one. A loyal servant to the Most High. A true servant of all Israel. A rare breed at most."

"Only due to this war."

"The war is not what I wanted. I came to Rehoboam and tried to get him to see reason. To not rule as his father ruled. Yet, instead he chose to follow Solomon's footsteps and in doing so, he has created a war. A war of two kingdoms."

"So, do I have your permission to sit with you and learn the ways you have learned?"

"Why not." Jeroboam turned to the soldier. "Grab this man a chair and leave us be. We'll be here for quite some time."

Jeroboam and Elrad sat down in the study as the king detailed everything to Elrad. From his time in Egypt and learning all he knows from Pharaoh Shishak. Elrad was taken away by what Jeroboam was describing.

"When I learned how Egypt was ruled by Shishak, he brought me into one of his briefings and it was unlike any briefing I've ever heard of or seen with my own eyes. There were no soldiers in the room. Only priests. But, these priests wore different garments than the Pharaoh. They seemed to be from other nations. Their speech was not Egyptian. They spoke of an agenda and how this agenda would cause the spiritual powers to rise from beneath the earth and aid them in battles, rulings, and in peace."

"I've never heard of something like that before." Elrad said.

"Most of the world have not heard of it period. Neither have many of the Israelites. I questioned how long this has been going. Pharaoh told me it was all happening when his father was in power and his father before. It goes far back in time. Before the Most High saved Israel out of Egypt."

Elrad listened more to Jeroboam's words of how the Pharaoh taught him the ways of a secret order. One eerily similar to the Order of Hunters. Elrad kept himself focused as Jeroboam would describe this order of worshipping a plethora of gods and all who were a part of this order were referred to as Priests. Shishak was the Egyptian priest and the others came from across many parts of the world. Jeroboam later described how he left Egypt after Solomon's death and he knew the prophecy would come to pass due to Solomon's rebellious acts against Yahweh in the form of building temples for idols in favor of his foreign wives.

"I see you were well-prepared for this." Elrad said. "For all of it."

"It is all in the will of Yahweh." Jeroboam added. "Now, I must continue with my business as usual."

Jeroboam stood up and went to the door with Elrad following.

"I thank Iddo for sending someone keen to understand my plight in this matter."

"He knows what's best."

"And where it comes from."

Elrad nodded.

"I'll leave you now, King."

"If you see Iddo, tell him I thank him for this visit."

Elrad left Penuel and made his travels back south. As he entered Shechem, he was greeted by Iddo, who was waiting for him near the entrance. Elrad stopped and stood next to the Prophet.

"Why are you out here?"

"To see if you have done what was asked and you have."

"I learned more than I was expecting to from Jeroboam."

"I see. You know where he's learned all knows. What the Pharaoh taught him."

"What of this other order? This Order of Priests?"

"Come with me."

Elrad followed Iddo to a home near the entrance to Shechem. There, the sun was slowly setting and Elrad needed the rest. Inside, Iddo and Elrad sat together as a handmaiden gave them food and water.

"The order in which Jeroboam told you is not the same as the Oth Tsayad. It is the opposite."

"Opposite in what way?"

"They are called the *Seder Kohen*. As I'm sure Jeroboam told you, they are an order of priests. All come from across the world. In joining the Seder Kohen, they all worship many gods. They also worship the spirits of the unseen."

"You're saying they do the bidding of the Adversary?"

"It is their purpose."

"And what is the Hunters'?"

"To eliminate the enemies which seek to destroy all that is good. Monsters, demons, and the like. They are enemies toward the Hunters. To the Kohen, they are all allies in this war."

"If we stop the Kohen, we can save lives."

"That is the objective of this cause. For many centuries have the Hunters fought to keep the balance in place. The Kohen are the ones who pull the cards of diversion and deceit."

"Now, shall I go and speak to Rehoboam?" Elrad asked.

"Go and speak to him. Finish your trials and all will begin."

Elrad left and traveled to Jerusalem where Rehoboam was dwelling. He arrived at the city and entered the palace. As he walked in, soldiers stared at him. Watching him like hawks. Elrad nodded to them in peace as he made his way to Rehoboam's throne room. Elrad entered and Rehoboam saw him.

"I've received word you would arrive."

"May I ask who told you?"

"A man of Yah."

Elrad nodded.

"Same with me. I guess we're here this day on familiar terms."

"So it seems." Rehoboam added. "Tell me, why are you here?"

"I've come to tell you that I am on your side in this civil war. Jeroboam seeks to do much harm to all of Y'israel and I intend on aiding you in stopping him. For your father's sake and his fathers before."

"I've heard the stories, that all of this is of my father's doing. His rebellion against the Most High has certainly shaped the kingdom and ripped it into two. Also, I hear this is what the Most High desired. Two kingdoms at war. Judah and Israel. Tell me, what should a man in my position do in such a cause orchestrated by the Creator himself?"

"I would obey to voice of Yahweh and take great heed to his word. Lead his people in the manner as your fathers before have done. To guard the commandments, statutes, and laws. To make sure your children and theirs after will have a kingdom to rule and to dwell in. not to end up as slaves to the other nations outside our borders. This is the way. This is the vision for the people. One of hope. One of honor. One of integrity. That is what I would suggest to a man in your place, my king."

Rehoboam nodded and looked over toward the elders. The elders stared at Elrad and looked at Rehoboam with a nod. Rehoboam knew the response and thanked them kindly.

"I must be grateful to have someone of your stature in both mind and spirit to be allied with the Kingdom of Judah."

"I go wherever Yahweh sends me."

Rehoboam thanked Elrad once more and the hunter left the room. From this point forward, Elrad was mentored by Iddo concerning the ways of the Hunter's Sign. Rehoboam and Jeroboam continued in their warfare as many Israelites are being killed in battle. Elrad assisted Rehoboam when he called for him. Elrad trained himself in combat and stealth tactics. Iddo taught Elrad the wisdom of the unseen. The ways of the Hunters. After several months, Iddo presented Elrad with several scrolls. The scrolls contained information concerning monsters, spirits, and demons which have been sighted and encountered across all of Israel and outside of its borders. Elrad studied night and day aside from training and assisting Rehoboam.

Jeroboam was told by his officials of Elrad's duties under Rehoboam and he shook his head.

"I knew he was that kind of man. He's one of them. A Hunter."

"What do you mean, sir?" A soldier asked.

"It's a secret matter. I'll deal with it."

CHAPTER EIGHT

Five years have passed since Rehoboam became king and now, the war had grown. The Kingdom of Judah had become a land of distain and deceit. Holiness was abandoned and forgotten as now the Kingdom was turned over to abominations and desolations. They built high places throughout the kingdom. Images and groves were also risen up and placed atop the highest hills of the kingdom and under every green tree that was possible. All of Judah did evil in the sight of Yahweh and in turn to their ignorance, Pharaoh Shishak was on his way to taken siege of Jerusalem.

Elsewhere in the wilderness, Elrad grew more into his calling of the Oth Tsayad. His knowledge increased as did his skill set. He spent more time in prayer and fasting. Mentored by Iddo continuously throughout the five years. Elrad would only enter Jerusalem on terms of business. He would not speak to anyone outside of his duties. He did keep to his word of assisting Rehoboam in his war against Jeroboam.

Eventually, the day had come where Shishak invaded Jerusalem with a massive arm of sixty-thousand horsemen, one-thousand two-hundred chariots, and four-hundred thousand infantrymen. The invasion came to a surprise toward Rehoboam and Elrad was present in the ongoing battle. Yet, there was hardly any fighting to be had. For Shishak took over Rehoboam's cities without a clash, leading toward Jerusalem as his final stopping point. On the field, Elrad had taken down some of the Egyptian soldiers and looked around for Rehoboam, but he was not on the battlefield. Instead, Rehoboam was crept up in his chambers, hiding from the Egyptian king.

Shishak had entered the temple, taking everything in his sight. He also took everything of value from Rehoboam's home. All of the gold and treasures were taken. Including the golden shields of Solomon. Shishak and his army left Jerusalem and the city remained standing, but it was looted of all that made it what it became. Sometime later, Rehoboam visited the looted temple and was ashamed of himself. He had the shields replaced with brass shields, a shame to himself and to the kingdom.

Elrad took the time to gaze at the temple before leaving Jerusalem. On his way out, he was confronted by Iddo, who questioned his current motives. Elrad had his horse ready.
"Where are you going?"
"Egypt. I must confront this Pharaoh."
"I know what has just transpired is a tragedy. However, this might make Rehoobam sober and turn back to Yahweh."
"That's not why I'm going."
"Then, why are you going to see this Pharaoh?"
"He's a member of this Kohen. An adversary to the Oth Tsayad. I cannot allow him to live."

Iddo nodded.

"I now see. You have more important matters to tend to."

"You comprehend them well. On the battlefield, I saw several shadows. They were not present before. They accompanied Shishak on his way here. He brought more demons to our land. Cannot let that remain."

"And when you do confront Shishak, what will you do then?"

"As any of us should. Kill him and move onward to the next."

"You truly are embracing the path."

"It is necessary. I now understand this. Perhaps, I will get more answers when I speak to this Pharaoh."

"Take care of yourself, Elrad." Iddo said. "May the Most High be with you."

Elrad nodded and rode off from Iddo and Jerusalem.

After his travels from the Kingdom of Judah toward Egypt, Elrad arrived in the city of Pi-Beseth, known in the Egyptian tongue as *Per-Bast*, a city known for its center worship of the goddess Bastet. Unknown to Elrad, a festival was taking place for Bastet. Men and women of Egyptian heritage rode on river rafts down the Nile as the men standing by played with pipes of lotus and the women on the cymbals and tambourines. Their culture was different to Israel and Elrad knew it well. It did not take the focus of the mission at hand from his mind. Several Egyptian soldiers stood guard, talking amongst themselves. Elrad leaned in closely from the nearby walls of a home, listening to their conversation.

"This is a celebration indeed." One soldier said.

"Ah. Bastet must be proud." The other soldier replied. "Did you see the Pharaoh anywhere? I was told he was here."

"He's at the temple. Has it to himself. Everyone else will be granted entry after."

Elrad received what he needed and made haste toward the Temple of Bastet. Crossing the Nile to reach the temple and as he did, he saw the cat statues of Bastet. Elrad shook himself to avoid the spiritual effects emitting from the statues. They had power and still do this day. Elrad was keenly aware. Elrad moved quietly around the temple walls, seeing only a few soldiers present, Elrad took a peek and saw Shishak, bowing own before the onyx statue of Bastet. Praising her for all she's done for him. Elrad entered the room and stood still. Shishak paused in is praise and stood up, turning around to see Elrad.

"Who are you?"

"A Hunter. Looking for his prey."

"Hunter?" Shishak noted. "Who are you and where are you from? Your speech isn't from our land. Wait, I recognize your garb. An Israelite. Here in Egypt. In my kingdom? In a temple of our gods?!"

"I know who you are, Shishak. Who you truly are and what you have done."

"Did Rehoboam send you here as a means of revenge for what I've done? I took everything from your god's temple and he did nothing in return. Is your god truly with Rehoboam? Is he with you?"

"You will find out, member of the Kohen."

Shishak paused. Elrad stood still.

"Kohen? You called yourself a Hunter. Who are you here to hunt? Me?"

"I know of the Seder Kohen. the order responsible for many of the spiritual ramifications across these lands."

"Ah. I see. I understand now. You're one of them. Those Hunters I've heard about in my time. There hasn't been one in this lands since the reign of Khufu. There isn't one of Egypt

41

any longer."

"I am the one within Israel."

"And you've come to kill me? To seal your allegiance to the cause of the Hunters. To rid the earth of the monsters and spirits which inhabit this and all lands?"

"I will do what I must. Jeroboam told me enough. How you taught him of the Kohen ways."

"And that is why he's succeeding in his war with Rehoboam. The Kohen properly know how to use the powers beyond for greater causes."

"It ends this day."

Shishak applauded Elrad's courageousness.

"I must ask, since you seek to eliminate the monsters and the spirits from the earth, though I am sure you've encountered your share in Israel. But, perhaps you should meet one of ours. See if you're truly capable of being a member of the Oth Tsayad as you claim to be."

Shishak chanted a peculiar spell, clapping his hands as the desert sands imploded into the temple with Shishak himself vanishing from Elrad's sight. Elrad used his diadem to cover his eyes and mouth from the rushing sands and once they receded, Elrad heard and felt the loud footsteps coming from in front of him. As he removed the diadem from his eyes, he saw himself staring in the presence of a manticore. The beast on all fours stood at the height of nine feet. It had the body of a lion with sharp talon-like claws on its feet and the face of a woman. Elrad had never encountered a beast such as this one. The manticore shrieked and stroke its paws against Elrad, slamming him into the temple walls. Elrad stood up, running on the piles of sand with his sword in hand. He swiped the beast on its legs as its spiked tail slammed down into the sand, attempting to impale him. Elrad moved over to the tail as it continued slamming and swiped his sword, cutting the tail from the beast.

"Let's see if you can conquer this one!" Shishak's voice echoed through the sands.

"Show yourself!" Elrad yelled. "Come out and face me. Don't use your monster as a cover!"

"I am among you, young one. You cannot see what truly is immortal!"

"You are but a man. Not a god."

"You do not know what you speak, Israelite. I am the Pharaoh! I am God in these lands!"

"And I have come to prove you wrong."

Elrad dodged his surroundings as the tail of the manticore continued to slam around him, digging into the sands. Erlad stopped in place and held his sword upward, he closed his eyes, keen for an attack. He stood for several seconds and the manticore lunged out from the shrouding sands, looking to attack. Elrad's eyes opened and with one sudden swipe of the sword, the manticore's throat was slashed. The beast fell into the sands and the rushing winds ceased. Elrad could see the surroundings again with Shishak staring him down from the column of the temple. The manticore shrieked in pain and Elrad approached the downed creature and raised his sword.

"Who are you supposed to be?! A hunter who only kills for his pleasures?!"

"This is who I am." Elrad said, slamming the sword upon the manticore, beheading the creature.

With the beast dead, Shishak went and grabbed his sword from the floor near the Bastet statue. He stepped forward with the sword in front. Tapping the tip of the blade to the ground. Elrad noticed him and walked toward the Pharaoh. Sword in front as well. Elrad was ready to fight. Shishak sought to eliminate the sudden threat of an Israelite in his country.

"You could abandon this sudden call of the Hunters and

align yourself with the Kohen."

"Why would I choose such a life to live?"

"The Kohen are the future of this world. No matter the kingdoms which rise and fall."

"Yet, ideals live on. Hunters will always remain as long as there's prey to find and enemies to destroy."

"You see. Remnants are as but a small fracture in this world. A replete, such as myself, will always be remembered. Our work will live on for generations to come. In a thousand years, men will speak of my name and my accomplishments. Ask yourself, will they speak of you and yours?"

"What I do this day will determine that future."

"Very well, Israelite. If the manticore was not enough to kill you, then I must complete the task myself."

"You talk of rhetoric. I have heard the stories of men like yourself. High and mighty in your position. Only to be taken down by those who you set to belittle."

Elrad ran toward Shishak and the two entered a swordfight. One of brutality as neither held back their offensive attacks when made an impact. Elrad was more offense than defense. Shishak was the opposite. Shishak went to trip Elrad, yet, he jumped as the Pharaoh's foot inched closer. Elrad shoved Shishak and swiped with his sword Shishak's chest. The Pharaoh paused, looking down at his chest, seeing small drops of blood on his tunic.

"Your good. Why stop there?!"

Shishak continued the attack, becoming aggressive with each strike. Elrad deflected the attacks, elbowing Shishak in the face and shoving him back. Elrad went for another swipe, Shishak caught the attack, kicking Elrad to the ground. Shishak walked toward him in haste, sword held above his head with a sinister grin on his face.

"I thought your Israelites were tough! Get up and fight

me!"

Shishak swiped the sword, Elrad dodged, rolling across the ground. He stood up and slashed Shishak's right thigh. Shishak laughed with Elrad confused to the laughter.

"Nice one."

Shishak went for another attack and Elrad deflected it smoothly. The Pharaoh went to make a step, but his leg was in severe pain that he fell to one knee. He looked up as Elrad approached him. Eyes were focused. Both of them. Elrad stood over Shishak with the Pharaoh laughing about the circumstance.

"If this is my end, do it now. Otherwise, I'll rise up and slay you here. Then, I'll return to your homeland and kill your brethren. Then, I'll take your women. Your children will forsake your ways and become adopted into the Egyptian way of life."

"You continue to talk as if you are the victor." Elrad noted. "Yet, you are down on one knee. Bleeding from the chest and leg. You are defeated, Pharaoh. You have lost."

"I have not. Neither has the Kohen. Repletes can always be replaced. My death won't change anything. All it will do is put out a signal to the others that the Hunters are out in the open once more. Then, you and your kind will wish you were dead after what the Kohen does to you all."

"Then, I shall await their visitations with my blade. You time on this earth is over, Shishak of Egypt."

Elrad impaled Shishak in his back through his chest. The Pharaoh fell dead on the temple grounds with his blood pouring out underneath him. Elrad cleaned his sword and sheathed it. He bowed is head toward the dead Pharaoh.

"May your gods be kind to you. Wherever you go."

The Pharaoh guards were heard entering the temple and Elrad made his escape as they found the body of Shishak, yelling for help as they carried his body out of the temple. In the distance near the Nile, Elrad watched, bowed his head once more and turned to walk away.

CHAPTER NINE

Elrad made his return and told Iddo all of which transpired. Iddo congratulated Elrad on learning ore concerning the Kohen and his complete sacrifice to joining the Oth Tsayad. Elsewhere, the civil war between Judah and Israel continued on with Elrad offering his support when it was necessary. Elrad never saw Rehoboam again after several battles against Jeroboam's forces.

After some time, Rehoboam had given up the ghost and now, his son Abijam would take his place as king over the Kingdom of Judah. Word had gone out concerning the death of Rehoboam and the succession of his son. Everyone in Judah mourned the death of their king, Elrad set himself apart from the others as the days of mourning continued for thirty days.

Once the days of mourning were complete, Abijam took full reign over Judah as his mother, Maachah stood by his side. Abijam's actions were not unlike his father. He followed in his footsteps completely. Doing all he had done before and the people complained over his ruler ship. The talks of being overtly strict and his ongoing wars with Israel. Elrad knew

Abijam would walk in the ways of his father, yet he knew that for David's sake, the Most High set up a son after him to establish Jerusalem as it should and shall be. In doing so of these events, Elrad took what he owned, which was not much and left Jerusalem, choosing to live in the wilderness over the sin-infested city.

Several days had passed in which Iddo visited Elrad at his small homestead out from the sights of Jerusalem. There was quietness and contentment surrounding Elrad's home. Iddo entered the home of Elrad, sitting down to eat and drink with him.

"I'm sure you're going to tell me how things are in Jerusalem?"

"As they've always been since the division." Iddo said. "Abijam continues his father's war against Jeroboam and Israel. Many of our people are dying by each other's hands. Neither side will listen to reason."

"And yet, they believe they're all hearing from Yahweh."

"That they believe. It's just, they need someone to follow. A true leader."

"Yahweh has that covered. You know he has someone already in place for when the time is appointed."

"However, such a season is yet to have come."

"And what will you do from now on till then? Give your advice to the young king?"

"I will do whatever Yahweh commands me to do."

Elrad nodded.

"But, you've done your best in aiding the Kingdom of Judah against Jeroboam's forces."

"I gave him my word that I would aid him against Jeroboam's forces." Elrad said. "Now, Rehoboam is no longer with us. My word is now in void. His son continues Rehoboam's foolish motives. I had to leave."

"That I know. But, what if Yahweh calls you back to assist Judah and protect Jerusalem from outside forces?"

"I will be there." Elrad confirmed. "No questions asked."

"Understood." Iddo said. "I have other matters to attend to in Yisra'el."

"There is something else. I did not know this Kohen was more spread out than before. It's not just Egypt they've infected, it's everywhere. Every known region to Man."

"The Repletes desire to take thrones and dominions over everyone and everything of this world. Remnants, such as yourself and those who've come before you, and those who shall come after, work in a much diverse way. You do not seek such things are carnal man does."

"How are we supposed to make change if not in the seats of authority?"

"By working in the way Yahweh works. It is mysteries to humans, yet, when you look at it further, it is not as mysterious as once before. He does his work in the midst of all. They neither see it, hear it. Nor can they smell or taste it. It is only when it has been completed that it begins to touch those in its presence. Your actions with Shishak are a primary example."

"What of the other regions out there? The nations? Yahweh does not care for them. That I stand by. But, they have demons of their own. Aren't there any who do the work for them as I am doing?"

"They have their Remnants." Iddo smiled. "Just as Yisra'el has theirs."

"Something has to be done." Elrad said. "What if I decide to head out into the nations. Clean them up of these monsters? What will come upon the world then? A better sense of peace or more terror?"

"Elrad, you cannot take it upon yourself to go out into the world and clean it up. There are others who are in those far regions doing the part of the mission."

"And I am the one in Yisra'el?"

"Precisely."

"I must ask, if there are others in every region, where was the one in Egypt? When I arrived, there was none. None to my knowledge at least."

"Not everyone gets a Hunter at the exact same time. For all you know, your actions in Egypt have already caused some major changes. Shishak is no more. Now, his son Osorkon rules in his place. Your actions have indeed brought the word of a Hunter to Egypt."

"If one does rise in Egypt, I hope to meet them. In the times ahead."

"It won't be the first of Egypt. But, only another."

"The first?" Elrad noted.

"He paved the way for many during the older days of Egypt. However, he was not one of us."

They continued to talk for several hours and Iddo left Elrad's homestead. Some time had passed, where Elrad traveled off toward south. On his travels, Elrad stopped and saw a notice stamped into a tree facing the main road. Elrad grabbed the notice and read it. The details written upon the scroll were descriptions of a strong demon causing panic in Beersheba. Whomever wrote the notice was begging for help. Help of any kind. Elrad, knowing his calling, took the scroll with him as he made his travels toward Beersheba.

CHAPTER TEN

Elrad made his arrival in Beersheba and without a moment's notice, he was bombarded with the townspeople, begging him for help concerning the demonic presence surrounding the area.

"Please, settle down." Elrad told the crowd. "Give some space for me to walk."

While making his way into the town, a woman approached him calmly, yet with intrigue.

"You're him."

"I'm who?"

"The Hunter."

"What do you mean?"

"You have to be him. You have the appearance of a striking one."

"I've come to help with the cause."

"You saw the scroll."

"I did. I'm here to solve the problem."

"Then follow me."

Elrad followed the woman into the town. The crowd dispersed from him as they approached a home. Elrad followed the woman inside, where he saw an elderly man sitting. The man's eyes glared up toward Elrad and brightened within. The woman walked toward the man and bowed her head.

"He's here."

"You've come." The elderly man said.

"I must ask. You've heard of me?"

"You're the one who killed Egypt's Pharaoh."

"How do you know of this?"

"Word spreads." The woman answered. "The description of the killer matches your physique."

"I see. I've come to help with the town's disturbance."

"You have come to rid us of the demon."

"I read the demon was a strong one."

"Indeed, he is." The man said. "His name is Asmodeus."

"Asmodeus?" Elrad said. "I've never heard of the name."

"Asmodeus is a powerful demon. He's come to cause havoc and spread fear throughout Beersheba. There was nothing we could do but pray to Yahweh for help. By our petition, He sent you."

"I see. Where was the last sighting of this Asmodeus?"

"He was seen at one of the homes near the edge of the town."

"I'll check it out."

"Best be careful." The woman said.

"I'll be protected."

Elrad left the home of the elder and traveled to the edge of town, where he discovered the homes were attacked by Asmodeus. When Elrad questioned the owners, he realized something particular with them all. Each of them were married and the husbands were harmed in the attacks. Elrad told them to stay away from their homes come nightfall as he was prepared to face Asmodeus. Later, throughout the day before night had come, Elrad set himself apart from the townspeople of Beersheba and prayed to Yahweh until dusk had peaked in. Elrad had sought wisdom on how to deal with Asmodeus and rid him from the land. Once, the sun had set and Elrad opened his eyes, he found himself surrounded by three men, dressed in priestly garbs.

"Who are you?" Elrad asked.

"We're with the ones whom you're against. We seek what you desire to take from us."

"Us?"

"We know what you are. A Remnant of the Oth Tsayad."

Elrad's eyes keened and he grabbed his sword and fought against the three men. Killing them with quick blows to the chest and neck. The three priests had fallen. Elrad took in their words more carefully, realizing they were part of the same group as Shishak. News of the Pharaoh's death had spread further than he realized and now he was a target of the Seder Kohen. Elrad cleaned his sword and removed the bodies from his sight.

After the fight against the priests, Elrad found himself standing in the presence of an angel. Strong in strength and might. Elrad moved back and stayed on his knees.

"Rise up, Elrad of Benjamin." The angel said.

"Who are you?" Elrad asked. "Have you been sent to help in this endeavor?"

"I am and I have. I am the archangel, Raphael and I have been sent by Elohim to assist you in your work against the demon Asmodeus."

"I praise His name. What must I do to cleanse this town of Asmodeus?"

"Head over to the waters of the river Tigris."

"Tigris?" Elrad said. "It will be daylight upon my return to this place. I sought to rid of Asmodeus this night."

"Asmodeus is not a low-level spirit. He is powerful and if you were to face him this night, he would overtake you and you would be defeated. Your duty failed and your life dust."

"I understand."

Elrad went up from his place and traveled to the river Tigris. There, he stood and a fish arose from the water, which Elrad caught with his bare hands. From there, Raphael appeared to him once more.

"Keep the fish, Elrad of Benjamin. For this is what you must do. Open the fish and remove its heart, liver, and gall."

Elrad did as the angel had said. Raphael raised his hand toward Elrad as he finished,

"Place them safely."

Elrad placed them safely in his gear and roasted the fish and ate it. Afterwards, Elrad fell asleep and arose just before dawn had set in. Raphael was there with him the entire time, watching over him. Elrad arose and asked Raphael concerning the heart, liver, and gall of the fish.

"The heart and the liver must be used to make smoke to expose the evil one. Such as evil spirits are. As for the gall, it must be used on the eyes of those who were harmed by Asmodeus' cunningness. To return sight unto them who have been wounded."

Elrad stood up, grabbed his gear and was ready to return to the site of the homes. Raphael knew Elrad's intentions and they were of a good nature. Therefore, Elrad traveled back to the homes, where the owners all came out, asking him questions concerning Asmodeus. Elrad told them he was met by an angel and the angel had prepared him for the fight against the evil spirit. As for those who were harmed by Asmodeus, Elrad used the gall to anoint them and their sight had returned to those who Asmodeus attacked. They saw the healing and praised Yahweh. This pleased Elrad and gave him more encouragement to confront Asmodeus.

While walking through the town, Raphael spoke with

Elrad and told him to grab the ashes of perfume from one of the wives' living at the homes. Which Elrad obeyed. He retrieved the ashes and Raphael appeared to him, stating this very night, he would confront Asmodeus and rid him from Beersheba. Elrad was ready and prepared himself by mediating and praying.

Once dusk had come, Elrad arose and the air was silent. He went to the homes and could feel a deep eerie presence surrounding them. Elrad entered one of the homes, placing the heart and liver of the fish upon a table. Following with Raphael had instructed him to do, Elrad took the ashes and laid some of it upon the heart and lings and set a fire to it. Causing a smoke to rise up in the area of the homes. There, a loud screeching was heard from above as Elrad gazed up, seeing Asmodeus flying over the land, seeking to retreat.

"Asmodeus!" Elrad yelled. "I see you now! You cannot hide any longer!"

Elrad grabbed his bow, yet realized a natural arrow would not pierce a spirit. As he placed his bow back, a calmness set over him as he saw Raphael fly above him and snatch Asmodeus by his neck and taking him away from Beersheba. Binding him and taking him far from the land of Israel. Raphael had returned until him the following day before leaving. From that very moment, Elrad knew this would be his lot in life. To face such threats which seek to do the Israelites harm. Only with Yahweh's aid can he achieve these feats of accomplishments. Elrad now began to embrace what he has become. A member of the Oth Tsayad.

CHAPTER ELEVEN

Sometime later after Elrad had dealt with Asmodeus, King Abijam had gathered the Kingdom of Judah together and went to Mount Zemaraim to face Jeroboam and the Kingdom if Israel. Abijam tried to gather all of Israel together, proclaiming Yahweh is their true leader. However, Jeroboam did not take heed to the words of Abijam and went to war with the son of Rehoboam. Abijam was well-aware of Jeroboam's attack and the armies went into battle with one another.

In the distance near the mountain, Elrad sat upon his horse and saw the battle commencing. Elrad no longer placed himself in political matters that were outside of his hand or purpose. Elrad shook his head in shame and gazed up to the heavens.

"How long will our people kill one another? How much bloodshed is needed to repent for past sins?"

When Elrad was looking in the sky, he caught a glimpse of something above him and the mountain. He keened his eyes, seeing the hovering figure. It appeared to be wheels within wheels, turning at a quick speed. Elrad saw eyes upon the wheels and they were looking down toward the battle. Elrad jumped off his horse, watching the object in the sky.

"In the Holy One's name, what are you?" Elrad wondered.

The object continued turning and bolted high in the sky above the clouds. Streaking like a lightning bolt. Elrad looked and saw it was gone.

"You were watching it all." Elrad uttered under his breath. "You know what's to come."

CHAPTER TWELVE

Elrad traveled to Jerusalem after the months had passed from the Battle of Mount Zemaraim. Upon arriving in the city, Elrad went into the caverns of the Well of Souls. There, Elrad stood alone and went down on both knees and prayed. He continued to meditate on all he learned from Iddo. He mediated on the ongoing war between the two kingdoms and what was to come of Israel's future. Elrad raised up his head, seeing the stone structure sitting before him.

"I now make this proclamation. I am Elrad. Born of the Tribe of Benjamin. Circumcised the eighth day. Taught in the ways of my forefathers. Instructed the ways of the Torah. Raised by a father who feared Yahweh. Nurtured by a mother who feared Yahweh. Now, I stand as a man. A man on my own. After what I have seen and heard from the divided kingdoms and the revelation of such secret groups, I now make this known before heaven and earth. I will protect all of Israel from the principalities and rulers of darkness in this world. This is my heritage and will be until the breath has gone from my body. I am no longer referred to as Elrad of Benjamin by my brethren for I am a Remnant. I am now Elrad, a Hunter of the Oth Tsayad.

A FIRST LOOK AT MARK PORTER OF ARGORON

CHAPTER ONE

United States Army Lieutenant, Mark Porter is currently on a mission to Roswell, New Mexico. Porter is 6'4, and 276 pounds, he has the full facial hair, beard and moustache, with shoulder-length black hair and stunning green eyes. He is courageous, honorable, and eternally optimistic, even in the face of Death itself. He's wearing his lieutenant uniform as he's traveling inside a black car, just him alone as he listens to musical instrumentals. As he drives, his cell phone rings and he answers it.

"Lieutenant Porter." he said.

"Porter, this is General Dunlap.' the caller said. 'How far are you from the site?'

"I'm looking at it as we speak.' Porter said.

Porter drove himself to the entrance gate, where two soldiers stood. They opened the gate for Porter and he drives through. Porter realizes the location, still speaking with the General on the phone.

"General, what is this place?" Porter asked.

"This is Area 51." the General replied.

"Area 51." Porter said. "I never thought I would be here."

"See you inside, Porter." the General said.

Porter hung up the phone and drives to the front entrance of the buildings. Area 51 has the appearance of a small city, with dozens of people throughout it. Most of which are military soldiers and scientists. Porter gets out of the car and walks toward the front doors, which are made of bulletproof glass. He walks in as he's greeted by soldiers and scientists. Porter makes a left turn to the elevator. He walks in and standing beside him are two scientists.

"Excuse me, but are you Mark Porter?" one scientist asked.

"Yes I am."

"It's an honor to meet such a well-known Lieutenant." the other scientist said.

"Thank you."

The elevator door opens and Porter is the first one to walk out, only to avoid the two scientists. Porter walks down a hallway and in the distance, he spots General Dunlap. Porter begins walking toward him. General Dunlap spots Porter coming down the hall near him.

"Porter, right on schedule." General Dunlap said.

"Yes sir, General." Porter replied.

Porter and General Dunlap walk toward another room. As they walk, General Dunlap begins telling Porter a few rules regarding him being there in the first place.

"Porter, there are some rules that you must obey, since you're here." Dunlap said.

"Ok, General." Porter replied. "What are they?"

"You must not tell a single soul what you're about to see in this next room." Dunlap said. "If you do, we will have no choice but to rid you of the world."

"I see. Must be something very important."

"Important?" Dunlap said. "Try highly secretive. If anyone found out about this, the world will turn for the worst."

They reached the room and the metal door slowly slides open. They walk in and the room is covered with military security and is dark with only little light inside. Porter looks around and sees scientists doing autopsies on unknown beings.

"General, what is going on here?"

"I'll tell you once we've reached our location." Dunlap said.

They passed the security and walk into another room. This room has plenty of light and isn't dark like the other one. Inside the room is a long table, with a device sitting in the middle. Porter and Dunlap walk over to the table and look at the device.

"Porter, this device you see here is able to transfer beings such as us to other worlds."

"How is that possible?" Porter asked. "Has it been tested?"

"Not yet. We're still awaiting answer from the President."

They walk around the table, looking at the device from all angles. The device is shiny and ejects a blue light that points into the air. Porter slowly puts his hand over the device. Dunlap snatches it from getting closer.

"Porter, you don't want to do something that you'll regret." Dunlap said.

"Sorry, sir."

As they stand, looking at the device, an alarm goes off. Porter and Dunlap look around. Dunlap walks toward the doors, asking the security what triggered the alarm.

"What the hell's going on?!" Dunlap yelled. "What triggered the alarm?!"

"The base, sir, its under attack!" a soldier yelled.

"Porter, stay where you are."

He pulls out his pistol and looks outside the door. From the outside, he sees soldiers and scientists being attacked by an unknown force. They appear to have tentacles, but are wearing white robes with long white hair. Dunlap stares out of the glass window of the door, looking at them and watching them kill the soldiers and scientists. Gunshots are heard from the outside, but they're dying left and right.

Porter walks toward the door, but is stopped by Dunlap, who commands Porter to stay by the table.

"General, what's going on?!" Porter asked while yelling.

"Sit tight, Porter. We're in for a show."

Dunlap backs from the door as it bursts open. He begins shooting at the beings, but the gunshots have no effect. Porter takes out his revolver and shoots one of the beings in the head, which kills it. Dunlap looks at Porter, astounded.

"Try that, General."

"I surely will."

They both begin shooting the beings that are coming into the room through the damaged door. They aim for the head and shoot them directly there. They've killed the beings and look at each other. Both astounded and calm.

"Good job, Lieutenant."

"Same to you, General."

They shake hands, but from the ceiling a bright light shines down on them and Porter pushes Dunlap out of the way and a loud bang is heard with a large flash of light, nearly blinding Dunlap. The light fades away and Dunlap looks around for Porter.

"Porter?" Dunlap said. "Porter?!"

Dunlap looks around and realizes that Porter is nowhere in sight, but he also realized that the device's light is now dim, which before it was bright. He now knows that someone has happened to Porter.

Porter, who's opening his eyes, realizes that he's in a desert. He looks and stands up, brushing the dirt off of his uniform. He walks around the area, looking around at it surroundings.

"Where the hell am I?"

He continued walking, but realized that he can move faster and jump higher than usual. He now knows that something isn't right. He continues to move ahead, but in front of him, he sees something running towards him. He tries to get a closer look and he sees that they aren't human. He begins running the other direction, but is shot down by a bow and arrow. Porter lays on the ground as the beings get closer to him. He now hears silence, but the beings are surrounding him.

The beings appear to be sixteen to seventeen feet tall and slim with green skin. They have no hair and only nostrils. They also have two eyes, four arms, and two legs. They look down at Porter as he looks up at them. They speak in an unknown language that he can't understand. He stands up, while staggering from the arrow shot, backs up from the beings and points to the one that's wearing white fur, who looks to be the general.

"You, where am I" Porter asked. "Tell me where the hell I am?!"

The being stared at Porter, looking at him as if he's not from this world. The being walks over to Porter and looks at him from all angles and stands back with his group. Porter stares at the group, reaching for his revolver, but he doesn't have it. He looks at the general being and it has his revolver.

"How did you get that?!' Porter asked with rage. 'Where am I?!'

Porter walks over to the beings, but he is knocked unconscious by one of their punches. They drag him back to their location and lock him up. Hours later, Porter awakens and is now chained to a rock with no way out. He sees the beings from before, but this time, there's more. Porter begins thinking that he may not be on Earth anymore. He know believes that he's somewhere else, somewhere unknown.

MARK PORTER OF ARGORON 2021

THE FIRST THREE STORIES OF

SYMBOLUM VENATORES

THE GABRIEL KANE COLLECTION

THE RISE OF THE MUMMY'S TOMB

1863

EGYPT EYALET

It is the beginning of summer as the Monster Hunter and Ufologist, Gabriel Kane travels to Cairo, Egypt by ship to investigate the Pyramids of Giza and the ancient tombs of the old leaders. He also seeks on discovering if extraterrestrials had any part in the construction of the pyramids and had any influence on the pharaohs of old. Even though it is at risk from the ruling Ottoman Empire.

Upon arriving in Cairo, Kane, wearing a brown hat and trench coat, he searches for a camel to use in order to gain access toward the location of the pyramids. He ends up finding a man who is selling camels and he approaches him.

"Camel will cost you." The Camel seller said.

"I know. How much for the camel?"

"I personally accept gold or silver."

Kane smiled as he pulled out five shekels of gold and three shekels of silver from his coat pocket. The facial expression of the

Camel Seller changed in an instant, showing excitement and shock.

"That will do, my good sir. That will do."

The Camel Seller accepted the shekels of gold and silver from Kane and gave him the camel. Kane mounted onto the camel and set his sights toward the pyramids that were in his eyesight within a distance.

"Move it." Kane said to the camel.

The camel began to move as Kane kept his eyes of the pyramids.

Kane continued his movement toward the pyramids as night immediately approached and covered him along with the landscape. Kane decides to stop and allow the camel and himself some rest before arriving at the pyramids, which are within a three to six-mile radius of his location.

Waking up along with the sunrise, Kane mounted back onto the camel and moved along closer to the pyramids. Kane raises his head upon entering El Giza, seeing the Great Sphinx in the horizon as he approaches the Pyramids of Giza themselves. Astonishing in some form by their height and size, he began to wonder how the structures were built and how much strength was needed to complete a task of that size.

Kane mounts off the camel and begins his investigation on searching and studying each of the three pyramids. He begins with the smallest one, known as the Pyramid of Menkaure. Already with the knowledge of the pyramids as tombs for the pharaohs, Kane searched the smallest one for any details concerning extraterrestrials either involved with the building or with the pharaohs themselves.

"I understand and know of the legend of Herodotus." Kane said. "Believing how Menkaure was more of a benevolent Pharaoh than the ones that came before. So, it may be."

Kane entered the mortuary temple of the pyramid and

discovered how the foundations of the inside were made of limestone. Kane glanced down at the floor and realized they were made from granite and had granite facing surrounding him by way of the walls.

"Judging by the minerals it took to build this thing, this must have taken a long time to complete and this is just the interior."

Kane looked and seen what appeared to be an inscription in the temple. Kane stared at it while deciphering the language. After deciphering, Kane understood the inscription stated that the temple was made as a monument for the Pharaoh's father, who was the king of upper and lower Egypt. While inside, Kane also discovered carved images of the old kingdom and understood it due to its high presence of evident details it held.

Kane continued his search of the Menkaure pyramid, before deciding that he should search the other two before the next nightfall. Kane continued his search with only a little water to drink and hardly ate anything before his investigation of the pyramids. Kane finished his search of the Menkaure pyramid. He set his sight on the second pyramid, known as the Pyramid of Khafre or Pyramid of Chephren. The second tallest of the three pyramids. Khafre is the tomb of the fourth dynasty pharaoh Khafre, who had ruled from the time of 2558 till 2532 BC.

The Khafre pyramid has the length of two hundred and fifteen point five meters leading to seven hundred and six feet. The rising height of the pyramid went from one hundred and thirty-four point four meters, equaling four hundred and forty-eight feet in height.

"Amazing are these structures."

Kane had understood that the pyramid may have been robbed ages ago and decided to head straight toward the burial chamber of the pyramid. Kane had questioned if the pyramid possessed two locations of entry, but he never figured it out to be exact. He continued walking until he had entered the subsidiary chamber.

Which had opened from the west of the lower passage. Kane believes the chamber was used to store precious items that belonged to the pharaoh or anyone close to him. The passage above appeared to be made in a clad of granite, which descended into a horizontal passage that lead Kane straight toward the burial chamber. Kane followed the passage directly.

Kane found himself standing inside the burial chamber. Kane looked at the size of the chamber and noticed it was carved from the bedrock through a pit. The roof of the chamber was constructed of limestone beams that appeared to have been gabled. Kane saw how the chamber had a rectangular shape and stared at the sarcophagus of Khafre. Seeing how his coffin was carved out of complete block of solid granite and how it had sunk into the floor. Kane looked down closer to the sarcophagus and seen what appeared to be small animal bones laying close to the coffin.

"Animal bones. Hmm."

Kane looked around and decided to leave the Khafre pyramid and to finally search the third pyramid, the largest of the three and the most known one of the three pyramids. Kane exited the Khafre pyramid as he stared at the Great Pyramid of Giza, also known as the Pyramid of Khufu or the Pyramid of Cheops. The Great Pyramid is the oldest of the pyramids in the Necropolis Giza area.

Kane searched the three known chambers of the pyramid. Going through the three of them in the amount of time he had left until sundown. The lowest chamber appeared to be cut from bedrock and laid where the pyramid was built, however left unfinished. The second and third chamber were the King's and Queen's chamber. Kane noticed that the pyramid was the only one to possess ascending and descending passages. The three smaller pyramids near the Pyramid of Khufu appeared to have belonged to his wives.

While searching, a loud bang had sounded from the outside,

gaining Kane's attention, he rushed out of the pyramid to the outside to see what caused the loud noise. Kane had exited the pyramid and found himself standing in the presence of an ancient Egyptian army with a living mummy in front of them.

"What is this?" Kane said.

Kane continued to stare at the Egyptian army and the living mummy that apparently led them. Kane slowly reached for his pistols on his side until the mummy took a step forward in front of him.

"Who are you and how are you even alive?" Kane said.

The mummy spoke in Egyptian and Kane could understand the ancient language the mummy had spoken. Kane gripped his pistols tightly, waiting for the mummy to strike with his army.

"You are Akhenaten." Kane said. "If that is the case, then why are you over here?"

"I am here to tell you to leave this land before the curse falls upon you and those that will follow you in the future."

"What curse will follow me into the future?"

"It appears as if you lack spirit and do not seek to understand the curses that dwell in this land. The curses that those before you in times past felt, the plagues that ran their course on this land and the curses of the ancestors that lived here in times past."

"You won't be able to fool me, Akhenaten. The curses will not affect me in any way because I know what is going on around here."

"Be that as it may, stranger. But I warn you to leave this land at once."

"So, I take it that this curse of a mummy's tomb is your doing. You're the mummy that folks say has risen several times and placed curses on those who entered this land in search of knowledge."

"I warn you to leave. This is your final warning, stranger."

"I won't leave." Kane said as he fired his pistols toward

Akhenaten and his army.

Akhenaten didn't make a flinch as the bullet flew past him without any harm. Kane continued to fire before placing the pistols back in their holsters as he pulled out his sword and ran toward Akhenaten. Akhenaten placed his left hand in front of Kane, shoving him back a few feet as lights shined down from the sky. Kane partially covered his eyes to see where the lights were coming from and seen three unidentified flying objects in disk shapes, hovering over the three pyramids of Giza.

"What is this?" Kane said. "The flying disks."

The sun had set, and the moonlight shined down upon the area. Kane looked above the disk and noticed the pyramids were in the exact alignment with Orion's belt in space.

"Interesting placement they did."

Kane turned to see Akhenaten, but he and his army had vanished without any noise being sounded. Kane turned back to the three flying disks as they began to levitate higher in the air and leave at warp speed. The sky was clear of the disks and silence filled the area. Kane nodded with his hat and turned away, seeing his camel still sitting in the same location as he left it. Kane makes the decision to leave the area as his theory had presented itself before him in the form of Akhenaten and the three flying disks.

THE UFO CRASH OF 1863
NOVEMBER 28 1863
AMERICAN CIVIL WAR

During the night, something mysterious in the sky is falling towards the ground. As it falls, it glows a reddish-green color and coming down faster and faster. It slams into the ground and is stuck there. The next day, Confederate soldiers discover the crash and take the object to one of their bases. Their leader, Robert E. Lee confirms that it was only a bombing accident but didn't tell them the description of the object. He commands his soldiers to take the object in their possession and to keep it highly secret.

On a ship, heading towards the United States, is Gabriel Kane. A monster hunter and ufologist. Kane is a man in his early twenties. Twenty-Three exactly. He's lean and gloomy, somewhat somber-looking at times for his age. His skin appears pale with his cold eyes. His face is shadowed by his hat. He is dressed entirely in black and is equipped with a weaponry that features a rapier, a dagger, a cutlass, a saber, and a pair of flintlock pistols.

He arrives in the United States to discover the crash site. As he travels across the northern lands, he runs into a group of confederate soldiers, who are weary of his presence.

"Identify yourself, sir." One soldier said.

"I am Gabriel Kane. Monster hunter and ufologist from Europe." Kane said. "I am here to visit the area of which an object crashed."

"There was no crashed object." The soldier said. "I believe you've been given wrong information. Now, return to your home."

"I don't live here." Kane said. "I came across the Ethiopic Ocean on ship. I heard directly that something fell from the sky around this area. So, that's why I'm here and my information is never wrong."

"This time it is." Another soldier said. "Now, leave this area at once, boy."

"Just tell me where the location is." Kane said.

One of the soldiers smacked Kane in the face with the butt of his rifle. Kane's head turned quickly before he wipes the blood off his mouth and turns to the soldiers, smirking.

"If that's how you want to play it." Kane said.

Kane kicked the soldier and knocked him to the ground. He looked toward the other two soldiers standing by, who ran toward him, Kane fired at them with his flintlock pistols.

Kane defeated the soldiers and continued looking for the crash site. As he continues searching the woods, he sees tracks on the ground in front of him. Kane walks over to the site and kneels, tracking the snow around the area. He looked up and spots something buried in the snow. He walks over and wipes the snow from it. It's a metallic object, a small, but heavy piece. Kane picks the object up and examines it. With his confused expression he says that this object appears not to be man-made. He puts the object in a small bag and continues walking toward the nearest town, just a few miles north.

Kane sees the town in front of him, surrounded with a few wooden buildings. He enters the town and sees the Union soldiers. Kane walks up to one of the soldiers and get his attention.

"Excuse me, but do you have any idea about the crashed object?" Kane asked.

"I'm sorry, sir. Who exactly are you?" The soldier asked.

"I am Gabriel Kane. I am a visitor from Europe."

"From Europe." The soldier said. "Why would you be in a place like this, especially during these times."

"I don't understand what you're talking about." Kane said.

"As of right now, we're in a civil war. North versus South." The soldier said. "See, me and the others you see around here are Union soldiers, the north. While the men in red are the Confederate, the south."

Another soldier in the distance calls out to the soldier speaking with Kane. He looks and tells Kane that he should look out for himself and that he might have to choose a side if he decides to stay a little longer. Kane looks on as the soldiers leave the town, heading into the forest. Kane walks through the town, looking at the buildings and certain areas. He sees both soldiers and civilians throughout the town. He decides to buy a map of the area and he looks through it. Going through the forest and heading to Adams County. Kane leaves the town and heads back into the forest, following the map.

Kane arrives west of the woods and discovers a frontier, surrounded and occupied by Confederate soldiers. Kane smiles at the sight of them, as if they're just targets to be taken down. Kane hides in the bushes to avoid any contact with the soldiers. He looks to his right and sees a group of them carrying an object of a large size, the object is covered with a blanket of sorts. The soldiers take the object into the large building in the middle of the frontier. Kane decides to sneak into the frontier, passing by soldiers swiftly. As he moves faster, he runs into a soldier.

"Who are you?" The soldier said.

The soldier took Kane's hat off and slammed it. Kane raised up and looked at the soldier. From behind Kane, more soldiers appear and eventually surround him. Kane notices that the soldiers are seriously hiding something due to their level of secrecy of hiding in the forest. The soldiers grab Kane and take him to the head center of the frontier. Inside the center building, sits Jefferson Davis. Davis sees the soldiers bringing in Kane.

"What are you doing?" Davis asked.

"We found him sneaking into the frontier, sir." The soldier said. "We caught him just in time."

The soldiers hold Kane in the center, facing Davis. Kane looks at Davis.

"What is your name?" Davis asked.

"My name is Gabriel Kane." Kane said. "I'm only here to investigate the crash that occurred in the woods."

"There was no crash." Davis said. "It was only an accident that happened out there. What could possibly crash?"

"There had to be a crash." Kane said. "I saw tracks and I found debris."

Davis stared deeply toward Kane. Staring him in his eyes with a slight confusion in his face."

"Debris? Of what?"

The soldiers let Kane go as he reached into his pocket, showing Davis the metallic piece that he found. Davis' face expression changes drastically, showing a sign of nervousness, along with an expression of anger.

"I found this piece in the woods, right around the crash site." Kane said. "The object was here in this spot."

"Ah! This doesn't prove anything!" Davis yelled. "Take him away."

The soldiers grabbed Kane by his coat and dragged him out. Once they reached the outside, Kane head butted the soldier and kicked the other one in the gut. Kane ran off into the forest as the soldiers began firing at him. Kane entered the forest and the soldiers run after him. Kane continues to run deeper into the forest as the soldiers track him by his footprints in the snow. As the soldiers follow the tracks, Kane turned left of the forest, his footprints disappear since there's little snow in the area. Kane continues moving and the soldiers lose tracks of the footprints.

"He couldn't have gone far." One soldier said.

The soldiers turn back and return to the frontier. Kane has now entered a complete grassy area, with only little snow. The sun shined down on him, as his hat have given him shade. As Kane continues walking, he looks at his map for the surrounding areas.

"Where am I?" Kane said, looking at the map. "What is this location?"

He looks at the grassy locations, not seeing nor hearing a single sign of life anywhere close. As he continues to walk forward, he spots a group of soldiers, wearing blue uniforms on horsebacks. Some are walking behind them. Kane stops and stands still as the leader of the Union soldiers comes toward him on his horse.

"Who are you, sir?" Kane asked.

"I am Abraham Lincoln." he said. "The President of The United States."

Kane is taken along with Abraham Lincoln and a group of Union soldiers to their frontier. Upon arriving at the frontier, Kane looked around the location, scouting the area for any sign of Confederate soldiers. Lincoln signaled to Kane to follow him inside the frontier. Kane followed him into the frontier.

While entering the frontier, Lincoln sat at a table and waved his arm toward the other seat which faced him. Kane looked and wondered.

"Please sit." Lincoln said. "We can talk right here."

Kane sat down at the table, facing Lincoln. Other Union soldiers walked in and out of the frontier. Many of them stayed outside guarding the location. Lincoln signaled the nearby soldiers in the frontier to stand guard outside, leaving him and Kane alone inside to discuss what's taken place. The soldiers exited the frontier leaving Kane and Lincoln inside at the table. Lincoln offered Kane some water and he took the cup. Both drank the water before speaking to each other.

"If I may ask, Mr. Kane. What were you doing out there?"

"I was running from some Confederate soldiers, sir. They were chasing me until I ran into you and your soldiers."

"When we found you out there, we didn't see any Confederate colors wandering about. So, why were they chasing you if I may ask?"

"I'm a resident from Europe. I came over here to investigate a crashed object that fell near this location. When I was searching for the object, the Confederate soldiers took me in and claimed that no object crashed, but I found evidence that goes against their words."

"Where is this evidence that you speak of? Do you possess it on you at this very moment?"

"I do."

Kane reached into his coat pocket and pulled out the metallic-like object. He handed over to Lincoln, who looked at it and rubbed his chin, questioning himself about the object. He handed back over to Kane, who placed it back into his pocket.

"I've never seen a texture like that in my lifetime. You believe the crashed object was made of that material?"

"Yes sir. I found this little fragment at the crash site. I didn't find the whole object. Someone took it and has hidden it from the eyes of many."

"I take it you believe the Confederate took the object and has hidden it from the people and mainly the Union. Might they believe the object could give them some form of extra help in this war that's taking place?"

"Whatever the case may be, sir. The object is not something to be toyed with. It possesses power of unspeakable energy. Energy that this world has yet to study and figure out."

Lincoln nodded while lying back in the chair. He took another sip of water from his cup and looked over at the door, seeing the soldiers walking about and keeping guard. He raised himself up from the chair closer to the table. He lies his arms across the table.

"I figure that you align with us and we can find this object you're speaking of. That way we will know for sure if the Confederates have taken it and are planning to use it for their own personal gain against us and the North. What do you say to that, Mr. Kane?"

Kane sat quietly, thinking to himself. He looked toward Lincoln and extended his hand. Lincoln extended his and both shook on the agreement.

"So, where do we head toward to find this object?" Lincoln said.

"We'll have to enter their domains. The only way to be sure about the whole situation."

"It's a fair start."

At a Confederate frontier, Jefferson Davis speaks with other Confederate soldiers about Kane's whereabouts. He questioned them on where he could have run off to and if he was a spy sent by the Union and Lincoln. The soldiers declined the statement and said he was only a man looking for the object. Davis walked out of the frontier and looked around the location. Giving himself some air from the inside.

"For goodness sake. We must find that man. By any cost."

Kane stood outside the frontier along with Abraham Lincoln discussing way of entering the Confederate frontiers. Lincoln gathered some soldiers to accompany them on their investigation. Gathering the soldiers, Lincoln considered the possible cost of having his men die because of a alien craft being hidden.

"I truly hope there's a craft." Lincoln said.

"There is a craft and you'll see it for yourself when we get to the destination."

"I believe your word, Mr. Kane."

Kane and Lincoln gather their supplies and head out for the Confederate base where the spacecraft is hidden. The Union soldiers follow them with their rifles in hand.

Upon leaving the base early on, Davis and a group of Confederate soldiers find a Union army base and immediately attack. Davis yells out orders to destroy anything and anyone they find within the base. The Confederate soldiers ransacked the base, destroying all that sits in the base. After the search, no Union soldiers are found by Davis and his Confederates.

"You cannot tell me that we've been made fools of." Davis said. "Where are they? Where could Lincoln be?"

Traveling a few miles from their base, Kane and Lincoln see a Confederate base in front. Kane sights no sign of Confederate soldiers nearby. He points out toward the base as Lincoln looks ahead.

"I see no bodies around the area." Kane said. "Shall we enter in?"

"Be cautious I warn." Lincoln said. "We don't know if this is a trap played by Davis and the Confederates."

They approach the Confederate base slowly, hiding behind the snow-covered trees and bushes to avoid possible sight. Kane looks around and sees no one, the area is as quiet to the point where only bird could be heard or the falling snow from the trees.

"This place is abandoned." Kane said. "We have our opportunity here, Mr. Lincoln."

"Where would they keep this craft, you speak of?"

Kane sees a large settlement ahead that sits near the back of the base. He points toward it.

"That's where it would be."

Kane mounts off the horse and runs toward the large settlement as Lincoln follows him and commands the Union soldiers to keep watch of the area in case Confederates appear to enter. Kane reaches the settlement and enters it and Lincoln looks around at the base before entering the settlement himself. Once they both entered, their eyes were locked on the craft, which sat on the ground in the middle of the settlement.

"This is it." Kane said. "This is the craft that fell from the sky."

"You were speaking the truth, Mr. Kane." Lincoln said. "Now I can see you're a man of your word and a loyal one."

"Don't give too much credit ahead of the victory."

Kane walks over to the craft and examines the encryptions and designs that are carved on the craft's surface and understands that it is an alien spacecraft. He pulls out his notes from his coat pocket and compares the drawings to the carved images on the craft. He sees that they are one in the same.

"This is an alien spacecraft indeed." Kane said. "There's more to the universe than what we know."

Kane and Lincoln immediately hear shots fired from the outside. They rush to see what's taking place and discover the Union soldiers firing at the Confederates that have appeared to the base. Lincoln looks ahead toward the entrance of the base and sees Davis with them.

"Men, we must leave at once!" Lincoln said. "We'll take this battle out into an open field!"

"You're planning on ending this now." Kane said.

"You don't have to stay with us any longer, Mr. Kane. You'll already found what you've been looking for and now you can continue on with your journey into the mysterious."

"No. You helped me and now I must aid you in your war against Davis and the Confederates."

Lincoln nods.

"Let's leave now!" Lincoln said.

The Union soldiers begin to leave the Confederate base. Davis shoves soldiers aside and sees Kane with Lincoln. He points toward them with anger in his eyes.

"There's that adventurer! He's traveling alongside Lincoln! I knew he was a Union soldier to begin with!"

The Union soldiers leave the base. Davis moves quickly to see where they're heading, and he spots an open field in front of them. He looks to his Confederate soldiers and hands them more rifles.

"We head toward that open field and we eliminate these Union soldiers for good and we take down Lincoln and this adventurer!"

The Confederate soldiers cheer as Davis leads them toward the open field. Kane looks back and sees Davis and the Confederates coming behind them near the field. He gets Lincoln's attention and points. Lincoln looks back and sees Davis coming. He smiles.

"Let them come and let them die."

Kane stands with Lincoln and the Union soldiers in the snow-covered field awaiting Davis and his Confederate soldiers to appear before them. The Union soldiers are ready for combat just as Kane and Lincoln are. In front they see Davis approaching and the Confederates at his back. Lincoln points out at Davis.

"This is the moment where this civil war will end." Lincoln said. "No more bloodshed upon this land amongst Americans battling Americans."

"Let's go ahead and finish this, Mr. Lincoln." Kane said.

The Union soldiers are ready as Davis and the Confederates face them. Both the Union and Confederate are opposing each other in the open field as it snows down above them. Davis smirks at Lincoln and Kane.

"I see you have the adventurer at your side, Abraham."

"I do and he is keen to do his work and move on from this."

"This is not his war. Its ours. The North versus The South. Nothing More. Union or Confederate and he made his decision to become a Union fool."

"We didn't want this war between us, yet you've asked for it and now you have it. For right here, it ends for good and there's no reason to continue this bloodshed on this land amongst Americans."

"Enough of your words, Lincoln. Let's get to the bloodshed."

"Suit yourself, Jefferson Davis of the Confederate."

The Confederate soldiers quickly run toward the Union, which do the same as Lincoln and Davis stand behind and watch the two armies run to each other in battle. Kane stares at Davis and glances at the armies battling it out amongst each other.

Shots are being fired and some are stabbed to death with blades. Davis looks at Kane and points at him. Kane spots Davis pointing and decides to approach him. Lincoln stops Kane as he walks toward Davis.

"What is it?" Kane said.

"Do not kill Davis. He's lost within his mind."

Davis looks ahead at Kane and Lincoln and laughs.

"Why are you holding the man back, Abraham? Afraid that he'll fail before you and give the Union a bad name on your expense?"

Lincoln looks at Kane. Concerned, yet trustworthy.

"Be careful."

Kane begins to approach Davis until the sky lights up above them and the battling armies. Kane looks up, holding his arm up to avoid the blinding light from above. What Kane sees is an alien spacecraft above the battlefield. Lincoln and Davis also spot the craft above them. Both are afraid, fear settling in their hearts at the sight of the large object.

"Oh my." Davis said. "It is real."

"What is it doing, Kane?" Lincoln said. "Why is it just sitting above us?"

"I do not know."

The craft begins to charge up as the sound of its engine begins to roar. Kane decides to get away from the battlefield. He pulls Lincoln alongside him.

"What are you doing, Kane?!"

"We have to get away from this area immediately! The craft is about to shoot down at us!"

Davis continues to stare at the craft, seeing its energy forming from beneath it. He is astonished at what he sees.

"Oh, how you can aid us in this war. The possibilities are endless."

The craft shoots down a beam of energy on the battlefield, separating the remaining Union and Confederate soldiers. Kane and Lincoln are behind a set of trees to avoid the blast. Davis is knocked to the ground at the impact of the beam. Kane looks up and sees the craft take off into the sky and it vanishes. The area is now quiet with a large burnt circle in the battlefield with melted and burned snow.

A few days later, Lincoln announces the civil war is still ongoing and the Union soldiers are preparing for more battles against Davis and the Confederates. Kane has taken the crashed craft with him on a ship as he returns to Europe to study the craft even more so than he could within the woods of a civil war going country.

THE UNDEAD AND THE EXTRATERRESTRIALS

1866

FEUDAL JAPAN

Three years after The UFO Crash of 1863, Monster Hunter and Ufologist, Gabriel Kane has now taken a trip to Japan to study of the ancient Japanese history and its culture. Now, during the final years of Feudal Japan. Kane is highly aware of its history and looks to discover more about it.

Kane, now twenty-six, three years after his involvement with the American Civil War, has learned a lot more about his occupation as a monster hunter and ufologist. Kane, wearing what appears to be a grayish-white trench coat and hat, with red Japanese markings on the coat, arrives at a small museum in downtown Edo. Inside the museum are dozens of artifacts containing amounts of history about Japan and the early years of Feudal Japan. Kane looks at one book and reads about its history.

"A very interesting history here." Kane said as he looked through the book.

Kane continues to look through the book and the museums, loud screams are heard from the outside of the museum. Kane, quickly turns and runs outside. Once outside, Kane sees a swarm of zombies. The zombies appear to be wearing ancient Japanese armor and gear. The zombies turn to Kane and run after him. Kane pulls out a sword and runs through the zombies, slicing them apart. As he slices through them, they spew out a liquid which is glowing green. One of the last zombies runs toward Kane, Kane moves toward the right and slices the head off the zombie's body.

After fighting off the zombies that surrounded the area, Kane kneels and examines the green liquid. As he gathers some in a small container for experimentation. Once, he stands up the Shogun military arrive. They stare at Kane, knowing that he's a foreigner. They walk over to him, speaking in Japanese.

"You are to come with us, sir." One soldier said.

"Very well." Kane said. "If you suggest it."

Kane holds his hands out as the soldiers handcuff him and take him onto their carriage back to their base.

Once they arrive at their base, they bring Kane, who's blindfolded, into a sort of interrogation room. They sit him down in a wooden chair and leave the room. Kane listens to see if anyone is inside the room. Hearing no sounds, he finds a way to take off the blindfold and looks around at the room. The room is completely covered with Japanese art from each wall. The room resembles a samurai dojo room to an extent. Kane looks behind him and sees the brown wooden double doors.

"Would like to speak with someone, please." Kane said, speaking in Japanese. "Anybody around here who I can speak with?"

Kane hears the double doors open, a Japanese man, wearing a white robe walks into the room with two Shogun soldiers. They stand on both sides of Kane as he looks in front of him, seeing the Japanese man.

"Do you really believe your staring will frighten me?" Kane said to the man. "I've come across worse."

The Japanese man stands silently while staring at Kane.

"For starters, where am I?" Kane said.

The Japanese man walks closer to Kane. Kane looks up at the man, seeing hardly any emotion in the man's face.

"You, sir, are in Edo Castle.' The man said.

Kane pauses as he begins to think. He looks at the man, startled.

"If we're in the Edo Castle, that makes you the Shogun." Kane said. "You're the military dictator of Japan."

"I am Shogun Yoshinobu." The man said, "The seventh son of Tokugawa Nariaki, daimyo of Mito."

"So, you're the current Shogun." Kane said. "But you said you'll never step foot in this castle nor Edo if you were Shogun. Why are you here?"

"I had to break my vow because of your troubles." Yoshinobu said. "For that reason, you must pay gravely and by gravely, I mean dreadfully."

Kane tries to break free of the ropes tied to his hands. Yoshinobu walks around him, quietly.

"You destroyed our test drill and that is why you must pay with your life.' Yoshinobu said. 'You've come into my country and disturb my governance.'

Kane continues to sit in the chair with his hands tied together behind his back as Shogun Yoshinobu walks around him in circles and later sits in front of Kane. Yoshinobu stares in the eyes of Kane, who does the exact same.

"Why don't you just kill me while I'm here." Kane said. "Because you know, I'll be out of here immediately within seconds."

"Your courage doesn't frighten me." Yoshinobu said. "Though my creations will certainly frighten you."

"Don't even bother trying to have your inventions to frighten me." Kane said. "Like I said, I've seen much worse."

Yoshinobu stood up.

"We know who you are, boy." Yoshinobu said. "You're Gabriel Kane, that monster hunter, ufologist man."

Kane stares at Yoshinobu.

"How would you have known?" Kane said.

"We've heard about your tale of being abducted by higher beings." Yoshinobu said. "We even heard about your tale in the Americas."

"So, I'm sure you know how that ended." Kane said.

"It doesn't matter how it ended." Yoshinobu said. "What matters is why are you in Japan to begin with."

"I was only here to study to country's history, nothing more." Kane said. "Why else would I be in Japan."

"Why did you destroy our Shogun undead?' Yoshinobu said.

"Excuse me?" Kane said. "What do you mean by your Shogun undead? You created those things?"

"We have such objects that can do a lot of things." Yoshinobu said. "We created them for a future military run. Today's event was only a test run, which your actions came along and destroyed them."

"You have no reason for creating zombies." Kane said. "What more could they do for you or your military."

"We can do so much more for our military." Yoshinobu said. "We've been doing very much so."

"I hope you and your country are enjoying your time in the sun. Because as soon as I get out of here, I'm exposing your plot and your reign will fall."

Yoshinobu smirked and began walking towards the door.

"We'll see about that, Mr. Kane. If you can escape this room anyway."

Yoshinobu leaves the room and locked the door. Kane turned his head towards the door behind him. He begins to move his arms around to let them loose. After moving left and right, he releases his left arm and lowers it towards his left leg. Reaching into his boot, he pulled out a blade and cut the rope from his arms and legs. Kane stands up and walked to the door. He tried to open it, though the door wouldn't bulge. Kane shoves his shoulder into the door three times. The door does not even move. Kane decides to pull out a small sharp knife from his coat pocket and jams it into the crack of the door. After shoving it through, the door opened as Kane jumped out of the room. He sees he's in a hallway covered with red, green, and white Japanese art and paintings.

"Which way should I go?" Kane said.

Kane chooses to head left in the hallway, passing by closed doors that could be a room like the interrogation room he was previously locked into. He turned down the hallway and quickly stopped as he seen two soldiers guarding a gate that leads into the other side of the castle. Kane slowly slips through the guards and finds himself entering the Shogun army base. He scans the interior of the base, noticing all the army's weapons and armor. Passing by one of the tables of weapons, he discovers two circular blades that look like two shrunken. He sees they have handles on the back as he pulled them, the blades quickly turn with a loud buzzing sound. Kane releases the handles and smiles.

"What a great invention."

Kane takes the blades and looked forward, seeing another door. He opened the door and sees numerous dead Shogun soldiers laying on beds and laboratory tables. Kane scans the bodies and notice their veins are glowing a greenish color. Kane's eyes squint as if he's seen the liquid before. He looks on the right side of the room, seeing a blanket covering a large object. Kane yanked the cover sheet off the object, revealing it.

"It makes sense now." Kane said. "Perfect sense."

Kane paused as he stared at a destroyed and somewhat damaged alien spacecraft. He walked over to touch the object but notices the green liquid that surrounds it. He backed up and looked at the bodies again, doing the math in his head, he realizes that the spacecraft liquid was used on dead soldiers to resurrect them as zombies. Kane searches the room to find a way to release the ship from its connection to the wall as its pumping the liquid into the dozen bodies of soldiers.

"How do I release this object from this wall?"

Kane reached to his right side and pulled out his sword and tries to swipe the long cable that its connected to the spacecraft to the wall. The sword doesn't leave any sort of mark on the cable. Kane pulled out two knives and tries to stab the cable from the wall. Not making any improvement as he tried jamming the knives in between the cable and the wall, Kane finally decided to use the Edo Blades. As he swiped the cable with left and right attacks, the cable suddenly gives loose, snatching itself from the wall as the spacecraft leaned and fell to the ground, causing a great disturbance to the soldiers standing outside the base.

Kane heard the footsteps of the soldiers entering the base and heading closer to the door. He searched the room for a way out and finds a small door to the right of the room hidden by a dirty brown curtain. He leaves out through the door just as the soldiers enter. Seeing the spacecraft on the ground and the cable cut from the wall, they sound the alarm. Kane tries to escape the castle's premises as he ran faster than he could possibly think. Though, he found himself surrounded by more Shogun soldiers, with Yoshinobu behind them.

"You thought you could easily escape my grips."

"It was worth a shot. Just wanted to see what you would do."

Yoshinobu looked at his soldiers. He nodded towards them and turned back toward Kane.

"Men, bring Mr. Kane to the dojo."

The soldiers snatch Kane by his arms and pull him into the dojo arena. They toss Kane in the middle of the room, facing Yoshinobu. Kane gets to his feet and sees he's surrounded by over a dozen soldiers, standing guard with their swords in hand. He looked at Yoshinbou, who's getting out of his robe, wearing a somewhat form of militaristic-martial-arts uniform. He grabbed his sword from the wall and approached Kane.

"I'll give you a chance. If you can defeat me in battle, I will let you leave the castle grounds and you can be on your way out of Japan."

"Very well. If that's what you want."

Kane stands face to face with Shogun Yoshinobu. Both have their swords drawn, facing each other. They began to circle each other as the Shogun soldiers stood still. Yoshinobu started to smirk at Kane, causing him to question the uncertainty of the battle.

"Well, are you ready to fall?"

"Only if you make the first move."

Yoshinobu swiped a rough swing toward Kane with his sword. Kane jumped back and slowly paused while he stared into Yoshinobu's deadly eyes. Kane moved slowly as he circled Yoshinobu, who did the same. The soldiers continued to surround them without making any moves or sounds. Kane turned to one soldier, who's holding a French rifle and swiped his arm, cutting it off.

"They won't even move." Kane said.

Yoshinobu jumped toward Kane with the sword in front. Kane swiped the sword with his own. Knocking it to the ground, Yoshinobu picked it up and raised the sword in the air, coming down like a strike of lightning. Kane held his sword up, blocking the impact of Yoshinobu. Kane struggled to hold back Yoshinobu's impressive physical strength. Kane noticed he was going down toward his knees as he couldn't fight off Yoshinbou's strength. He pushed back, slowly rising above Yoshinobu. As he faced Yoshinobu in the face, he kicked him in the abdomen, knocking him back.

"You decide to use your own body?" Yoshinobu said.

"In a fight, you use all that you have."

Yoshinobu dropped his sword and kicked it toward the wall. He began to set up in a pose as Kane stared. Yoshinobu moved swiftly as he kicked Kane in the face, knocking him into the soldiers. Which the soldiers shoved Kane back towards Yoshinobu, who proceeded to pummel Kane with various martial arts techniques of punches and kicks. Yoshinobu raised his elbow up above Kane's back and slammed it down. Kane fell to the ground in massive pain. Spitting out blood, he laid on the cold and hard wooden floor as he looked at Yoshinobu standing above him with his sword.

"It would seem you're not a great fighter, Mr. Kane. To which you appear to be much weaker than what the stories have told."

Yoshinobu raised the sword above Kane's throat. As he drove the sword toward Kane, he moved and kicked Yoshinobu from behind, knocking him through the window and outside. The soldiers began to move towards the window. Jumping through it and going to the outside, Kane proceeded to follow them. While outside, Yoshinobu noticed that most of Edo's civilians were standing by, staring at their Shogun. He yelled at them in Japanese to return to their homes. Kane jumped out of the window behind Yoshinobu. The civilians were covered with fear as they stared at Kane.

"So, you want to continue this battle?" Yoshinobu said.

"I plan on defeating you in front of your own people. To show them that even a leader of a country falls."

Yoshinobu ran toward Kane. Making a variety of attacks toward him. Kane dodged the attacks and backhanded Yoshinobu, who turned around as he held the right side of his face. He rubbed his lips, seeing blood on his hand. He turned to Kane with a fire in his eyes and he ran back toward him. He continued the attacks toward Kane. Getting a few jabs and haymakers in on Kane, Kane kicked Yoshinobu in the stomach and punched him in the face, knocking him to the pavement. Kane looked up at the civilians and turned to the soldiers.

"This is your Emperor."

As the civilians stared, an abrupt sound of distant groans began to approach their location. Civilians began to run as a horde of zombies approached the location. The Shogun soldiers ran over and began fighting off the horde. Swiping their heads and arms off with their swords and firing at them from a distance with their rifles. Other soldiers were ambushed by the zombies. Two zombies spot Kane and Yoshinobu. As they approach, Kane went back into the dojo, picked up his sword and ran back through the shattered window and began cutting off the heads of the zombies. Yoshinobu looked up and seen the horde of zombies against his soldiers, as well as Kane fighting a few of them off. He got back to his feet as Kane turned toward him.

"What are you staring at, Yoshinobu? Aren't you going to fight?"

Yoshinobu didn't say a word and walked back into the dojo. Kane shook his head as he continued to fight off the rest of the zombies. Many of the soldiers were killed by the zombies or by the green liquid that dripped from their decayed bodies. After the fight, Kane returned into Edo Castle and grabbed whatever was left of his gear and decided to leave Japan.

Upon leaving Japan, the following year, Kane discovered that Yoshinobu had retired from being the Shogun of Japan and wasn't seen by anyone of the public eye again. He also found out that it was the last and final Shogun, thus making it the end of Feudal Japan.

HOD

PROLOGUE - THE MURDER

The forest was cold, snowed in, and completely iced over. The atmosphere would cause a person to shiver in their footsteps to even taken the daring chance of walking through the forest covered in snow. Especially during nightfall where the forest would become silent as the outer depths of space. No sign of any animals either. Complete quietness.

Though, there was that one time during the night, when a man decided to take the daring opportunity to enter the snowy forest during a full moon. The man seemed to make an impression on his friends and possible lover. He took pleasure in taking those daring actions that many seem to do today. His dare was to enter the forest during nightfall and overcome the cold and shivering atmosphere.

Not even wearing a coat, he went out with only a short sleeve shirt and shorts. He might've had wore sandals, but we couldn't tell due to the fact that when we found him, he was halfway eaten and his feet were bare, his clothes ripped with claw marks and bite marks. His friends didn't know what to make of their friend's death and were too afraid to tell anyone of his daring feats.

We spoke to his friends concerning him and they hardly spoke a word besides the fact of him running into the forest with a smile on his face. The detectives however believed it to be a bear that attacked and killed him. But a hunter who discovered the remains believed it to be something more than a bear. Funny enough, one detective joked that it might have been an elk that killed him and used its antlers to create the claw marks.

"No elk could've done this." said the Hunter. "I can tell you exactly what killed this man. But, you'll end up locking me behind a steel door."

"Tell us what could've killed this man."

"A full moon was out on the night he entered these woods and we know the legends of this land."

"We are not buying this folklore tale of a werewolf being responsible, sir."

"Just hear me out, detectives. I know this sounds crazy, but you have to believe me and take this in."

"We prefer not to."

The detectives would laugh in the hunter's face and walk away to their vehicles, preparing to leave the forest and head back into town. The friends had already left the scene with little tears in their eyes and softness in their hearts. Without any ideas as to who or what might have killed the man in the snowy forest, the detectives were out of options. Until that Sunday, where the freezing rain had begun to come down and when he entered through the doors of the detective building that they knew something was happening in those woods.

I - THE INVESTIGATION

After a series of days had passed away, the detectives took slight heed to the warning of the hunter concerning the possibility of a werewolf as the culprit of the forest murder. Everyone within the small town kept the information of the murder to themselves, most were afraid to speak to someone about it. The hunter stayed in his cabin outside of the small town to avoid certain mockery and scrutiny. He was already the laughingstock of the town months back dealing with his hunting of deer to the point where deer figured out the shooting grounds of the hunter, thus never making a return to the field.

The hunter sat alone in his cabin, covered in snow. Placing wood into his wood stove to heat up the cabin, he sighs while sitting down in an old beaten chair. The hunter's cabin is covered with trophies he acquired in hunting games. The cabin is even packed with stuffing of his kills, ranging from deer to bears to an mountain lion. He reached over to a table nearby and grabbed a book, began to read it until a knock comes from the door. Reluctant to answer the door, believing it to be a towns person coming over to mock him or throw snowballs at him.

"Go away." said the hunter.

They knock again with the hunter's patience being tested. He refused to stand up and answer the door. Going back to reading his book, he ignored the door and the knocking.

"I am not in the mood to be playing with snowballs.

Thank you."

The knocks continue and increase. Nearly out of patience, the hunter stands up and walked to the door. He took a peep outside through the peek hole, seeing a man standing there. The hunter gently sighs before placing his hand on the doorknob. He opened the door and standing there is a man dressed in amalgam of modern and Victorian era clothing. The man is wearing a black duster coat, a gray buttoned-down shirt with black slacks, black and gray leather boots, and a black hat. The man's black and gray hair strands down to his shoulders, covering his ears. The man stands still while the hunter thinks to himself as to who the man could be.

"Hello, sir" The hunter said. "How can I possibly help you?"

"I heard about the murder in these woods. I understand that it was you whom discovered the remains of the victim."

"Yes. Yes, I did. Is there something wrong?"

"I would like to talk to you about it."

"I'm not in the mood to speak on the subject, sir. If you want more information on it, go to the detectives' office and they can give you all the information that you'll need."

The hunter proceeded to close the door, but the man placed his foot in between. Frightening the hunter immediately, he opened the door wildly.

"Sir, whatever you want, just take it."

"I don't want anything of yours. I only want to speak with you."

"About what? I told you where to go about the murder."

"I'm not here about the murder. I'm here about the werewolf."

The hunter paused and slowly took the time to regain himself back to normal, he calmed down and allowed the man to enter his cabin. The man entered and looked around the interior of the cabin, sighting the stuffed animals and trophy mounts.

"You are a hunter I can see."

"I am. Do you want anything hot to drink?"

"Do you have any coffee available?"

"I do."

"I'll take some of that. Thank you."

The hunter pours a cup of coffee for the man and brought it over to him. Giving him the coffee, he sits in his chair as the man sat in the opposite chair. The man took a sip of the coffee as he looked at the hunter.

"What can you tell me of the werewolf?"

"I didn't see the creature. I only brought it up as a possible suspect in the murder. The victim had marks on his body that were made by an animal and it couldn't have been made by a bear. The marks were too detailed."

"The bite marks and claw marks were very distinctive is what you're saying?"

"They were. I tried to tell the detectives, but they tossed the idea away. Blaming it on a bear in these woods."

The man nodded as he took another sip of the coffee.

"By the way you've spoken, you know a lot about werewolves I presume."

"I've heard about the legends. The transformation of man into beast. I've had family that have told me they've seen werewolves around this forest and in town. A legend that lives this long cannot be made of folklore tales."

"No. They cannot."

The man finished his cup of coffee and stood up, walking to the door. The hunter stood up and followed him. The man opened the door, taking his steps outside.

"Thank you for the coffee. You've shown me compassion."

"Where are you headed? If I may know."

"I'm going to speak with those detectives you've said. I

want more information on the victim."

The man stepped outside of the door, walking in the snowy grounds. The hunter watched and he wanted to say something, it sat on the tip of his tongue.

"Pardon me, sir. But I would like to know your name. You didn't tell me your name."

The man turned and faced the hunter. He stared at him for quite a moment.

"Hod." The man said. "You can call me Mr. Hod."

The hunter looked on as Mr. Hod walked away from the cabin and into the forest. The hunter closed the cabin door and sat back in his chair and continued the reading the book he had placed on the table.

In the small town, the residents walked around the area, buying from local shops and selling from local shops. Many of whom only spoke about business ventures and homesteading as they refused to bring up a conversation about the murder and the mentioning of the werewolf. While the residents were doing their daily business, they spotted Mr. Hod walking into the town.

All the residents stopped what they were doing and only stared at him. Hod kept to himself, avoiding eye contact with the residents. He walked through the streets. Residents began to talk amongst themselves as to who Mr. Hod could be.

"Why's he wearing those clothes?" said a man.

"He looks dirty." a female said speaking with a friend.

"He scares me." a child said.

Mr. Hod looked around the small town and found the detectives' office and proceeded to approach it. The residents would move out of his way. Avoiding contact with him period. They continued to stare at him and make comments pertaining to the way he dressed and look as far as he appearance was concerned. Hod found himself standing in front of the detectives' office. The building was entirely made up of wood and stone. He walked up the steps of the office and entered through the door as the residents walked closer to the building.

Inside the detectives turned and stared at Hod, who stood by the door looking at them. One detective approached him, shaking his shoulders with a thrust walk, trying to intimidate Hod, but he was unshakable.

"What can we do for you sir?"

"I came here to speak on the matter of the forest murder."

"Why is that? You know the animal that did it? Or did you do it?"

The detectives laughed slightly at the detective's remark.

"I know the animal that killed the person."

The detective chuckled as he walked toward his office. Hod followed him. The detectives look on at Hod, confused about his choosing of apparel, stating it looked too ancient for their time.

"So, you found the bear that did it?"

"Wasn't a bear, detective."

"A mountain lion is what you're telling me? I thought were rid of those damn things around here."

"Neither was it a mountain lion?"

"Well, what the hell could it be?"

"The victim was killed by a werewolf."

The detective slowly turns to Hod and stared.

"You haven't been around that lone hunter, have you? Because if you have, maybe his fanatics and kookiness have rubbed off on you."

"I did speak with him and no. His fanatics have not rubbed onto me. But, they have given me insight onto this town of yours."

"Listen, sir. We aren't listening nor buying into some children's horror tales. We have our own fictitious troubles to deal with around here."

"The werewolf is no fabled tale. Of course, it has its place in ancient folklore, but those folklores are based on actual events that have taken place ages before our time."

"How would you know any of this to be true? You're part of the government's secret agency or something?"

"What I know, the government would kill, rape, and slaughter anyone to find it out for themselves."

"I'm sorry. But we're not listening to any werewolf stories here."

"I have a proposition for you, detective. You and this entire town of yours."

"Which is?"

"I will find the werewolf and I will kill the creature. After which, I will leave this town and never bother to return."

The detective looked at his colleagues, who were also silent and were unable to come up with anything to say to Hod.

"So, when you kill this werewolf you're talking about, you want some reward before you leave?"

"I want and ask for nothing in return for the werewolf's kill. As of right now, I ask to see the victim's remains."

"The remains are nothing but bone and torn muscle."

"The remains have clues that contain where the werewolf has headed and will strike next. Show me where the body is."

"The body is kept at the morgue across the street. You can go there and ask for the remains. They should let you see them."

"Thank you for the talk." Hod said as he nodded with the tip of his hat.

Hod walked to the office door and exited, leaving the entire building of detectives silent. Outside of the office, Hod walked down the steps and through the crowds of residents that surrounded him and watched him approach the morgue. Before he entered through the morgue doors, a young girl approached him. He looked down at her, noticing her smiling, but could sense her fear of him from within.

"What do you want, little girl?"

"Why are you wearing those kinds of clothes?"

"Because, the clothes present what I am and where I come from."

"So, you're old?"

"You could say that."

"How old?"

"Older than you can possibly count."

"Oh…." The little girl said.

Hod showed a faint smile before entering the morgue while the residents continue their frightening stares. Hod opened the door and entered the morgue building. He glanced around the room, searching for someone inside to speak with concerning the body of the victim. He spotted no one inside the room until he took a few steps toward a door and it opened. Out of the door walked out the morgue attendant, who was frightened for a bit at the sight and presence of Mr. Hod. Slowly shivering.

"What can I help you with, sir?"

"I'm here to see the remains of the victim that was found in the forest."

"Why would you want to see that?"

"Because my purpose here requires me to take a small study of the remains to understand what committed the murder."

"So, you work with the detectives?"

"I work alone. I am not from around here."

"But, how would you get the right to come here and solve a murder that doesn't concern you. You're not even from here and you want to solve this. Why?"

"The murderer is known throughout the lands. I came to this dead house to see the remains to uncover more of what I need. I know what killed the individual in those woods."

"We all know it was a bear that killed him."

Hod stared at the morgue attendant. Silent and showing no emotion on his face.

"A bear was not responsible for the murder."

"Then what could possibly have the strength to do such a thing?"

"It was a werewolf and apparently the people here seem to keep quiet about the lore of werewolves. As if you're all trying to hide something that cannot be hidden no longer."

"We refuse to speak of such folktales around here. We don't want to frighten the children and spread fairy tales across the town."

"By lying to yourselves, you already have."

The attendant leans her head down, facing the floor as if she's in shame of Hod's words. Hod approached her and raised up her head and stared, slightly encouraging her to spread the truth about the werewolf lore.

"Show me where the remains are, and I will be out of your sight."

The attendant nodded slowly. "This way."

Hod followed the attendant through the door and walked down a quiet and cold hallway heading toward the chamber. While walking, the attendant was hesitant to bring Hod into the chamber, fearing he could kill her and run off with the remains. Hod didn't say a word. Hod continued to follow the attendant down the hall and kept to himself.

"I truly hope this is not some form of small-town trickery. Because if it is, not only will this attendant be shown the truth. Those standing outside these walls will surely know what is going on in their town. Whether they decide to believe it or not. She's walking quite slow, possibly in fear of me or what I could do. Makes no sense as to fear me. I am here for a purpose, not an assault."

The attendant reached the chamber doors and opened them as a cold breeze swiftly went out through the opening. The breeze touched Hod, gently touching him on his face. The cold had no chilling effect on him as he kept to himself and walked into the chamber. He looked around and seen the amount of bodies that were laying on the tables. Many of them appeared to have animal-like marks on their bodies.

"The remains are over here, sir."

"What happened to these people?"

"I fear they suffered from the same animal that killed the man in the forest."

"How long has this been going on for?"

"Almost three months now."

"The detectives don't do anything about this. Who's in charge around here?"

"The detectives don't like it when we bring it up. They're owned by the upper-class elite. They control most of what goes on here. The finances, the news we receive, and so on."

"Where can I find your elite class?"

"I, I do not know, sir. They keep to themselves and appear as they please. We only answer to them. Most of us here don't even question them out of the fear of death."

"Seems to me that there's been enough death going on around here to worry about your own selves."

The attendant walked over to one of the walls and pulled out the table, where the remains laid. Hod walked over and looked at them. Pulling out tools like a forensic scientist. He glanced at the remains and took deep looks at the bones, the muscles, and the skin fragments that remained. The attendant stood by and watched Hod study the remains in every detail that he possibly could. Using a magnifying glass to look closer at the bite marks within the bones. Hod looked around and didn't see the skull.

"Where's the skull?"

"This is all that remained."

"They didn't find the skull?"

"It is possible it's still out in the forest. They won't go back and check. They told us this is all they needed to start their search for the killer."

Hod pushed the table back into its closing and closed the chamber door. He walked out of the room and back down the hallway. The attendant tried to keep up by following him because of him power walking.

"Wait. Where are you going?"

"I am going into the forest to find the skull. When I do, I shall return here and deliver it to you to compete the remains. Without the skull, I won't have all the information I need."

Hod walked out of the morgue with the attendant looking nervous as to what could come up between Hod and the skull. Outside, Hod noticed the number of residents that stood outside of the morgue had increased. They stood around him, making way for him to walk by. The residents stared at him as he kept to himself.

"Who do you think you are." A man said. "Why are you here trespassing our town. We don't need foreigners like you around here."

Hod stopped and turned toward the man. The residents took a few steps back to avoid being in Hod's eyesight. He kept his attention focused on the man who appeared to be a farmer as he wore a farmer's garment.

"Trespassing your town. How could I do such a thing when I am here on duty."

"We don't know who you are. Hell, we've never even seen you before. You must be some guy from the outer borders of the forest."

"I am from the outer borders and once again, I am here on a duty. Not a vacation. As I told the attendant inside the morgue, you, townspeople live in an area of lies. You all know the truth and refuse to believe it and accept it. You'll rather live in a world of make believe than live in a world where the truth reigns. The truth of the matter is that it wasn't a bear that committed those acts of slaughter in the forest. It was a werewolf and the beast is still out there."

"You can't talk to us like that! You're not even a resident of this town. You have no right to speak to us in such a manner!"

"I have spoken. When I return from the forest, if I am to see you or any of these people again. I will speak once more. Your detectives won't solve your problems for you and now I will solve this one problem as it affects more than this measly little town."

Hod walked away, heading toward the exit of the town into the forest. The residents stood watch and looked at the farmer. The farmer looked around and glanced at his fellow towns people.

"Don't you even dare look at me like that! I was standing up for you people and what do I get? No respect, no aid, not even another voice to stand up with mine own."

Hod continued walking through the snow-covered ground as he entered the forest. The sounds of people form the town began to fade away as he went deeper into the forest. Hearing nothing but silence and a few specks of bird in the sky flying over the trees. He looked around in the snow, searching for the spot where the victim was killed.

"By the look of the snow, the victim's final place of living isn't far from this particular spot. Its closer than it appears to be."

Hod walked past the pair of trees and spotted claw marks in the wood. The claw marks were dug deep into the wood. He rubbed the wood, searching for something that could be remaining inside. Hardly finding anything, he pulled out a knife from his coat and started to slice the tree in the areas of where the claw marks were stamped. Slicing and even cutting through the wood, a small object fell out of the hole and into the snow. Hod stopped what he was doing and placed the knife back into his coat. He kneeled and searched in the snow to find what had dropped from the tree. He picked up the small object and looked closer at it with his magnifying glass.

"The object is a piece of a nail. The werewolf must've broken it off when it dug into the tree. Possibly at the moment of pouncing the victim. By the look of it, the beast is very strong and could've possibly killed the man with just the force of its lunging toward him."

Hod turned around and looked in front of him about a few feet away and seen dried blood in the snow. He walked over to it and rubbed the blood.

"This is the spot of the victim's fall. Now, where is his skull?"

Hod began digging in the snow with a pair of branches that were laying in the snow nearby a tree. He dug until he could see the dead grass underneath the snow. He continued digging in the surrounding areas and couldn't find the skull. After several minutes of digging, Hod stopped and looked around to see anything sticking up in the snow.

"Where is it?"

Hod started to walk and noticed something in the snow that laid in front of his left foot. He dug into the snow at the exact spot and instantly seen the eye socket of the skull. He reached down and pulled the skull up from the snow and wiped away the snow. He placed the skull into his bag and proceeded back into town.

II - THE BLUE MOON

While the sun was preparing itself to set away from the town and night was slowly approaching, Hod entered the town with the skull in tow. The residents returned and followed him back to the morgue. He didn't look back at the residents as they slowly followed him and were almost on his back. They noticed the bag and tried to take peeks to find out what was inside. Hod grabbed the bag and held it tightly to his chest and maintained his focus.

"I ask of you all to leave the bag alone and let me be."

"We only want to know what you have inside."

"An important object in finding the werewolf."

The residents stopped walking and stood still as they watched Hod enter the doors of the morgue. The residence kept to themselves and not even one of them spoke a word as they went back to their regular business. Hod entered back into the morgue and the attendant seen him come through the door and approached him.

"I take it you've found the skull?"

"I have."

Hod placed the bag onto the table and pulled out the skull. He handed the skull carefully to the attendant who placed it next to the remaining parts of the victim's body. She scanned the remains in full, trying to sort out the possibilities of the victim's body. Mr. Hod carefully examined the body himself. From the skull to the feet.

"What do you perceive now?" The attendant said.

"I perceive a full evaluation of the victim. There could be some werewolf venom in the bones."

"We can do a search through the bone marrow."

"Let's give it a test."

Hod and the attendant did their part of the test runs. Operating as best as they could.

"I'm sure you heard about the other cases besides the one in the woods."

"What other cases?" Hod wondered.

"There was a couple that was attacked, and a pair of bankers ambushed in the streets."

"I was not aware of such events. Were these before this recent one?"

"Yes. All the bodies had similar marks to this one here. I'm not sure what kind of animal would do such a thing so discreetly. But I'm hearing a lot about werewolves. So, I'll take what I can get."

"Believe my words, werewolves exist, and they come in all shapes, sizes, and forms. Some are just wild beasts, others intelligent creatures."

Upon the work, they discovered the venom of the werewolf indeed remained inside the bone marrow. Yet, when removed, the venom glowed a bright blue. Its hue was brighter than the lights in the room. The attendant stepped back from the table as Hod kept his gaze upon it. Before quickly covering the glow with his hand.

"What was that?"

"Spirituality." Hod said. "A powerful one."

While the attendant gathered the venom, Hod glanced toward the window and saw nightfall had arrived and the moon's light glistened upon the clear barrier between Hod and the outside.

"How are we going to tell the detectives about this?"

"Tell them." Hod said, his eyes locked on the outside.

"What will you do?"

"Find the creature. Night has come and it's out there. Lurking. Waiting."

"You said the light from the venom was spiritual."

"Which means we're dealing with a spiritual werewolf."

"I don't understand. I've never heard of such a thing."

"Spiritual werewolves are rare. Very rare."

"As in treasure rare?"

"Rare as in Eden rare." Hod proclaimed. "Either the creature came through another dimension or from worship. Doesn't matter. I will find it."

Hod left from the morgue and went outside. Walking towards the woods. A loud screech echoes through the surroundings. Hod stopped in his tracks, circling the area, listening to the scream. Tracking its whereabouts and without notice, Hod ran toward the sound and found himself running deeper into the town and as he reached the source of the scream, he stopped and could only stare.

"What is this?" Hod uttered.

Standing in front of Hod was a deceased woman and on top of her, gnawing at her throat was the werewolf. Tall, grey-haired, and brute size. The werewolf stood up, facing Hod. The werewolf let out a howl and the color of the moon transformed into a blue moon. Hod looked up, seeing the change in color.

"What are you?"

The Werewolf roared at Hod. Moving his hand to the side, pulling out a revolver and firing toward the wolf, which runs from the shots. Hod went and chased the beast into the woods. Hod stopped near the entrance and mediated. Looking at his revolver, he nodded and reloaded.

"I have to stop this."

III - THE LIGHT OF THE MOON

Hod entered the forest in search of the spiritual werewolf. Following its tracks in the snow at every turn, except for the moment where the tracks are nowhere to be found. Not even a scratch mark in the snow. Hod continued moving through the woods, hearing the faint sound of howling in the distance. Covered in the trees.

"I know you're here." Hod said.

From the distance, the werewolf lunged out at Hod. Its fangs sharp and pointed. The hair of the wolf glistened in the moonlight. Hod moved quickly and took a shot, missing as the werewolf returned to the trees in the distance. Hod breathed quietly while continuing to aim the gun.

"Just one time."

The werewolf lunged once more toward Hod, the gun was raising as it fires, hitting the wolf in the left shoulder. The werewolf slips in his steps and tumbles down to the snowy ground. Hod runs toward the beast, which swipes toward him with his right arm, Hod fires another shot as the wolf lets out a screeching howl. Hod sighs, lowering the gun slowly.

"That's it."

The moonlight looms over the wolf's body and from it rises a spirit. The spirit startles Hod without question, yet with curiosity in his cold eyes.

"What is this?"

The spirit flows higher into the air, passing over the trees and vanishing into the night sky. Later, Hod returns to the town to tell them of the news. The werewolf is dead, but the spirit still wanders.

"What must we do now?" A civilian asked.

"Take care of yourselves." Hod replied. "My work has just begun."

Hod left the small town of Rosebane. Returning to the lair of the *Symbolum Venatores*, the monster hunters within the shadows of the world.

Hod will return...

**NEXT CHAPTER IN THE
SYMBOLUM VENATORES SERIES:**

SYMBOLUM
VENATORES

twilight of the gods

2021

ENTER THE HISTORY OF THE HUNTERS

SYMBOLUM VENATORES

ABOUT THE AUTHOR

Ty'Ron W. C. Robinson II is the author of several works of fiction. Including the *Dark Titan Universe Saga* series and *The Haunted City Saga* series. Also of other books (*Frightened!: The Beginning, Lost in Shadows. Remastered, Accounts of The Dead Days, The Book of The Elect, etc.*) and One-Shot short stories More information pertaining to the author and stories can be found at darktitanentertainment.com.

Twitter: @TyronRobinsonII
Instagram: @tyronrobinsonii

Twitter: @DarkTitan_
Instagram: @darktitanentertainment